THIRTEEN

by Tom Hoyle

Holiday House / New York

Copyright © Tom Hoyle 2014
First published in the United Kingdom in 2014 by Macmillan Children's Books, a division of
Macmillan Publishers Limited
First published in the United States of America in 2015 by Holiday House, New York
All Rights Reserved
HOLIDAY HOUSE is registered in the U.S. Patent and Trademark Office.
Printed and bound in December 2014 at Maple Press, York, PA, USA.
www.holidayhouse.com
First American Edition
1 3 5 7 9 10 8 6 4 2

Library of Congress Cataloging-in-Publication Data

Hoyle, Tom.
Thirteen / by Tom Hoyle.—First American edition.
pages cm
"First published in 2014 in the United Kingdom by Macmillan Children's Books, London"—
Copyright page.
Summary: Targeted by a dangerous cult, thirteen-year-old Adam must save himself—and
the rest of London—before the New Year begins.
ISBN 978-0-8234-3294-3 (hardcover)
[1. Cults—Fiction. 2. Survival—Fiction. 3. London (England)—Fiction. 4. England—Fiction.]
I. Title.
PZ7.1.H69Th 2015
[Fic]—dc23

2014028416

prologue

In 1982 a sixteen-year-old boy from London was taken into care after attacking his parents. The boy's bedroom was filled with books, films and essays about the devil. One scribbled page had the title *The Great Book: A Prophecy.*
The boy's name was Michael Brown.
In 1996 he changed it to Coron.

By 1999 others were being drawn to Coron's message. At first, a handful of adults. Then more. Soon after, children began disappearing from the streets of London; many became members of the cult known as The People.

By 2013 Coron's Great Book ran to 1,138 pages. The following lines were underlined thirteen times: "By the time he is fourteen, the boy has become a man.... Thirteen is the last year of childhood.... The boy must be killed before he is a man."

part one

1

A man clasped the sharp end of a sword, raising it above his head. The blade cut into his hands, sending a web of blood down his arms and across his T-shirt. Drops fell onto the cold tarmac of the hospital car park.

In the distance a group of kids could be heard singing rowdily. It was the last five minutes of the millennium: 11:55 p.m. on Friday, December 31, 1999.

The man edged the sword higher, upright, far above his head. He muttered what sounded like an incantation, then strode toward the bright lights of the entrance.

Inside the hospital, four floors up, a young mother was giving birth. A nurse and a doctor stared at the tiny head that was emerging. "Well done. Keep pushing. That's it. Push hard."

The mother gave a growl-like scream through her teeth. "How much longer?" she moaned.

"Nearly there. One more push."

Shoulders appeared. Then a tiny chest.

Fireworks crackled outside, and waves of cheering echoed through the windows. Singing could be heard from somewhere within the hospital: "Should auld acquaintance be forgot, and never brought to mind...." Then, "Happy New Year!" The deep chimes of Big Ben drifted in from a television nearby.

Finally, and quickly, the rest of the baby boy slid out.

The nurse lifted Baby Adam onto his mother so that she could hold her damp, bawling son. His fingers curled around hers as he calmed, listening to her heartbeat.

"Well done, Kylie. You have a gorgeous, healthy boy," the nurse said.

The nurse looked down at her watch. She wrote some details, then added another line: "Born exactly at midnight at the start of the new millennium." The doctor gave a cheerful farewell and quickly left the room, pleased to be able to join the celebrations outside on the ward.

The newborn nestled into his mother's chest, and she held him close. Kylie was very young, still only sixteen, and not entirely sure of the identity of the boy's father. She smiled, happy for the first time in weeks, and tickled the baby's cheek with her knuckle. The birth had been easier than expected, and on exactly the due date, just.

There was another burst of noise from outside: giggling nurses flirting with a couple of grinning doctors. Fireworks continued across the city, just as they did up and down the country. Closer, Kylie heard another noise, faintly rising up through the lift shaft outside her room.

Four flights below, in the entrance hall of the hospital, a man was striking wildly at the button for the lift with the hilt of a sword.

Thump. Thump. Thump.

Crack. Some plastic shot across the tiled floor. Two nurses were calling desperately for security—one on the phone to the police, the other pleading, "Help! Someone help!" over the loudspeaker. But the usual security guards were not there; they had gone to watch the millennium celebrations on the television in the storeroom.

"Stay away from me!" the man shouted, holding the sword in his left hand.

The lift arrived—an elderly man in a wheelchair ready to

emerge. The sword was pointed erratically at him as the doors opened, and then at the terrified porter accompanying him.

But the man with the sword wasn't interested in them, so as they edged warily and desperately out of the lift, he pushed his way in and saw what he was looking for: Level Four, Maternity. He pressed the button, leaving a red smear on the panel, and the doors closed.

In the entrance hall the nurses and the porter watched numbly as the lift ascended, the numbers lighting up in turn: one...two...three...then, at four, it stopped.

Maternity.

In the lift the man transferred the sword to his right hand.

Thomas, the porter on the maternity ward, stood next to his empty trolley, waiting for the lift and quietly humming to himself.

Inside the lift the man prepared murder. *Kill them all*, he thought. *Like Herod. Sacrifice them all.*

The lift doors parted.

Thomas's punch arrived as soon as the doors were fully open. He saw an intruder with a sword, and that was enough. His fist hit a combination of jaw, teeth and lip.

But it made little difference. Although the man fell back against the rear wall of the lift, the sword didn't leave his hand; he lunged at Thomas, slicing a gash in the flesh at the top of his left arm.

The lift doors closed, trapping Thomas inside with the intruder.

As Thomas put his right hand to the wound, he was head-butted. Blood seeped through his fingers and dripped down his face. He fell back against the lift buttons and slid to the floor.

The doors opened again.

The man with the sword stepped out into the corridor, nudging the trolley out of the way.

A nurse appeared in the distance. "What the hell...?"

Sword and man stalked up and down the corridor, searching. He was not interested in the ward itself—only the delivery rooms, the ones with babies in them.

The man spoke to himself as he threw open doors. "Not that one. No. No." These were empty. He knew what he was looking for.

Then he returned to the lift, where the trolley stood in front of the metal doors. There was a room opposite. He pushed down on the handle, but the door was locked. Inside, nurse and mother and baby had heard the commotion and were cowering together in the far corner, trying to hide.

"This one. Yes. This one." He shoulder-barged the door. Then again—cracks appearing near the doorframe. On the third push the handle and fixing splintered, and the man fell into the room.

Nurse shielded mother, bravely, keenly, self-sacrifice and glorious headlines filling her mind. Mother shielded son, terrified, distraught, confused. The tiny boy cried.

Anger and hatred dribbled and spat from the man. He shouted loudly, his words like a bass drum, "Hand the Imposter to me! He. Must. Not. Live."

Then, even louder:

"HAND HIM TO ME. HE IS EVIL!"

Kylie couldn't think. Couldn't speak. She tried to hide, tried to hide her son, tried not to be so completely paralyzed by fear.

The man's voice changed as he moved toward them, now speaking quietly and calmly. "Okay. Then I will kill you all."

Kylie couldn't take her eyes off the sword, smeared, from tip to hilt, in blood.

Suddenly, Thomas appeared at the door and rushed forward in a blur, grabbing and pushing, wounded and wild. The two men stumbled toward the window, locked together; the sword fell to the floor and spun around and around until it stopped under the bed. Then they smashed against the large window that occupied much of the outside wall, their struggle lit up by another burst of fireworks in the night sky.

It was an old hospital, and this window had been on the repair list for some time. The combined weight of two heavily built men was enough to force the entire window from its rotten frame, showering glass down the side of the building and leaving Thomas holding tight to the other man as they balanced precariously on the very edge. Two policemen and several doctors and nurses rushed into the room, then came to a halt at the sight of them.

The oldest of the doctors, a tall woman with flowing ginger hair, spoke to Thomas. "Mr. Macfarlane, pull him back in."

The policemen stepped forward to assist as Nurse Bunce, Kylie and Baby Adam stayed in their frightened huddle by the side of the bed.

The man leaned back, pushing his center of gravity beyond the edge of the building, then, by forcing his arms sharply upward, snapped Thomas's grip from his T-shirt. Thomas snatched at him, trying to regain a hold, but though his fingers grazed the sword man's jeans for a second, he couldn't grasp him. The man fell backward, eerily silent, his eyes locked on Thomas, who had been grabbed by a policeman.

The man sliced through the branches of a large oak tree that reached up towards the window.

Snap. Snap.

Crack. Crack.

Thud.

Smash.

Silence.

The policemen and Thomas looked down from the window, unable to see properly through the tree and the billowing gloom fed by firework smoke.

Five minutes later, six policemen, led by Detective Inspector Grey, ran around the building to where the body had fallen.

Three ambulances were parked under the tree. The one in the middle had its blue lights smashed. Grey stepped forward, his shoes crackling on colored glass and flecks of wood.

"Give me a leg up," he told one of the policemen.

"Yes, sir. Would you like me...?"

"No. I'll do this, thank you."

Detective Inspector Grey rose slowly. Fearing the worst, he warily glanced on top of the vehicle.

In the middle was a deep dent, part of a large branch, and a carpet of twigs. But no body.

Fireworks fizzed in the distance.

And, in the confusion of millennium night, the man with the sword was gone.

2

FRIDAY, APRIL 21, 2000

The Master spoke in a whisper: *Find the Baby. Find all the Babies.*
Coron closed his eyes and nodded. He pressed his hands together. The scars hurt, but Coron liked the pain. He would kill again on Friday, April 21, at the ninth hour. Three o'clock in the afternoon.

Three o'clock on Good Friday.

From the air, the tower blocks looked like neat Legos, but close up they were chaotic: graffiti-covered lifts and passageways, windows boarded up with cheap plywood, stairs fouled by a mix of pale litter and stale urine. The block, Bakunin House, was to be pulled down in six months—in the meantime, only the desperate remained.

On the fifth floor, halfway along the concrete-gray passageway, behind her watery yellow curtains, was Kylie.

Baby Adam yelled and shrieked. He screamed with hunger and itchy discomfort. A gray toy caterpillar peered down at him like an angry snake. Three jars of baby food, a smear of green sludge left in each, sat on the table.

Adam howled. The same sound, over and over: *Waaa.* This wasn't the desperate sudden cry of a child in pain; it was the bawl of a confused baby. The same sound, over and over. *Waaa. Waaa.*

Kylie put her head in her hands and started to cry herself. In time with Adam, she sobbed.

A rusty fridge rattled in one corner. It was 1:30 p.m., and Kylie was suddenly hungry. The only food was a packet of ham, the only drink a can of Coke.

Waaa. Waaa. Waaa.

Kylie opened the red, thinly built cupboard and dragged out a glass. She opened the can and poured some into Adam's bottle.

Then she stopped and slumped to the floor, her head filled with tentacles of noise which grabbed hold of her brain and squeezed it tight.

Waaa. Waaa. Waaa. Waaa.

She held the glass tighter and tighter and felt that the noise would make her brain bleed.

Adam kept on crying.

Kylie sat on the dirty kitchen floor, feeling desperate, and thought of killing herself.

But then something deeper stirred within her. If she died, Adam would die. She had to get him away from here. Away from *her*. So she wrote the words *His name is ADAM* on the back of an old lottery ticket and tucked it inside his top.

Shivering, Kylie dragged Adam from his cot. Immediately he stopped crying, but the noise still surged through his mother's mind.

Kylie opened the front door and took short, old-woman steps down the passageway and stairs. Then she turned left out of the car park and reached the main road. She had to give Adam to someone who could look after him.

Kylie drifted over the curb and a car hooted at her, its driver glaring and shaking his head as he passed.

Kylie stumbled on, her mind whirring. Who could take Adam? And then, an answer. A big building with lights. A hospital? Possibly. Probably.

Kylie crossed the divided highway, not waiting for the lights. More horns blaring and drivers swearing.

Kylie walked on, oblivious. As she crossed the last lane, an Audi driver looked up from fiddling with his radio. He hit the brakes and swerved, smashing his side mirror on the truck beside him. Plastic flew into the air, and one of the larger pieces hit Kylie's shoulder. But still she walked on.

Confused, unaware of where she was, and almost totally unaware of what she was doing, Kylie left Adam on the steps under the lights, next to the large wooden sign. At exactly 2:13 p.m. she pushed Adam gently against the back of the step so that he did not roll away.

A short while later, a loud knock, more like a thud, came on Kylie's door. It was 2:50 p.m.

"Open up. It's Social Services." It was a woman's voice.

Kylie was slumped on the sofa. The empty can of Coke lay on the floor, alongside Adam's baby bottle. She didn't know what she was doing, or where she was—she just knew she didn't want to live any more.

"Open up. Social Services," said the woman again. *THUMP. THUMP.*

"Open up!" This time it was a man.

Kylie shuffled toward the door, bewildered.

Outside stood two neat figures. Kylie only noticed details: a golden butterfly brooch on the woman; a brilliant white shirt on the man. One of them spoke, but Kylie wasn't sure which: "We have come for the baby."

Kylie laughed. It was a helpless flare of laughter that shot out from deep inside her. She laughed and laughed, without a smile. "I have given my baby away." She spat out the words madly. "I haven't got a baby anymore."

The two visitors stepped into the room. The woman immediately went to the empty cot and said, "It's true. He's gone."

The man spoke. "Where have you hidden him?"

Kylie's mind was a smudge.

The man spoke again. "You'll find it easier if you tell us now."

Kylie's eyes wanted to close. She could only see fragments: a jar of baby food, a knife with brown sauce on it, the scars on the man's hands.

She had seen this man before. In the hospital. The man with the sword.

The woman closed the door and stood in front of it.

The man slowly put down his bag. "Kylie. I have been sent to find this child, and I will not disappoint my master. You will tell me where he is." Desperation erupted inside him. It was nearly 3:00 p.m. "TELL ME." He stepped closer. "HE. MUST. DIE."

Kylie thought it was all a nightmare. *I will wake up soon.*

Then she was forced to the floor, his hand digging into the back of her neck. "YOU will die."

But Kylie couldn't answer what he asked again and again, because she didn't know. She couldn't think, couldn't tell him, no matter what he did.

She died thinking that someone had come out of that brightly lit building and picked up her baby. She died thinking that Adam was safe.

She was right.

3

MORE THAN THIRTEEN YEARS LATER: WEDNESDAY, SEPTEMBER 18, 2013

Adam looked at his science results. He knew what the graph was meant to do, but the thermometer was not cooperating. The mercury stubbornly refused to go above eighty-five.

Turning to Megan, he mumbled, "This water is boiling like mad, so I'm going to say it's reached a hundred degrees."

Megan, on his left, had a neat collection of crosses in a straight line. Adam's graph looked like the outline of a deformed camel. He took another piece of paper and drew his crosses so that they made the shape of a smiley face, then placed it on top of Megan's sheet.

She smiled and shook her head slightly.

Then Adam drew a graph for Leo, on his right. It was clearly in the shape of a pair of breasts. Leo spluttered.

"Adam!" hissed Megan in warning as Mr. Rugg, the science teacher, drifted near.

But Adam had lost interest in the task. He had the two cleverest people in the class on either side of him—a wonderful opportunity to discover the right answer. He flipped open his textbook to the biology section. There was a picture of a peculiar-looking fish. "That's you in the morning," he said to Leo, who chuckled.

Megan looked at the picture. It did bear a passing resemblance to Leo.

There was a pause as Adam flipped to a page featuring an octopus. "Hey, Meg—look. This creature's amazing. It says here it has eight testicles."

Megan whacked him with her exercise book. "*Tentacles!*"

"I know!"

Leo laughed, half at Adam, half at Megan. Mr. Rugg didn't hear, but Jake Taylor did.

Returning from elsewhere in the room, Jake stopped at the end of the row and yet again punched Leo for no reason.

Leo pushed his lips together, keen not to antagonize Jake, who walked on.

Adam frowned and turned around. "Why did you do that?"

Jake had forgotten about Leo already and was saying something out of the corner of his mouth to the boy on his left. They were laughing in a cold and humorless way. Jake had already turned fourteen and was several inches taller than anyone else; his voice had broken, and he even had the hint of a moustache.

Adam felt anger stir within him like a deep rippling pool. Why did Jake want to spoil their fun? He stared at Jake and spoke louder: "Why did you do that to Leo?" Leo was one of the good guys, awkward and odd, but good. In need of protection.

Jake heard Adam over the hubbub of the classroom and raised his middle finger, but subtly, dismissively, as if an automatic, lazy response. He mouthed words at Adam: "Leo is a fat sack. I'll do what I like." Then he smirked and nudged his right-hand neighbor, a boy with a square face and gray eyes; they were staring at Megan's chest as she put her thermometer back in the box.

Jake's sniggering and muttering made Adam's anger more forceful and energetic, a fountain rather than a pool. Jake was unreasonable, nasty. Adam felt as if he was having an allergic reaction.

Mr. Rugg said something about the experiment, but it was

all a haze to Adam. The words *One hundred degrees is boiling point* stared down from the whiteboard.

Adam wanted to calm down; he wanted this sudden anger to go away. But it was like gravity—hopeless to resist. He stood up. Five strides later, he had reached Jake and hit him. No one had noticed Adam leave his seat, not even Megan. A single spurt of blood shot out of Jake's nose and onto the science book on the desk: page twenty-eight was later given an arrow and the words *Jake's blood.*

Jake fell from his chair and everyone else in the room backed away as Adam stood over him. Megan closed her eyes and breathed out deeply.

Mr. Rugg dashed from the front of the room to restrain Adam. He wasn't a big man, but he was wiry and probably would have been good in a scrap himself. But the moment had passed for Adam now—his anger evaporated as quickly as it had arrived.

Jake squealed his innocence from the floor. "I was just getting on with my work and this idiot came over and thumped me. He's probably broken my nose." He wiped his face and held out his hands as if in surrender. "What have I ever done to him? He needs to get his head examined. Typical—no wonder his parents gave him away."

Adam said nothing. His head felt as if it was full of porridge. He had never done anything like this before.

Mr. Rugg marched Adam out of the room. Mr. Sterling, the deputy head, was just passing, as he always seemed to be when least wanted. He looked through the glass strip in the window and shook his head at the situation. Jake was inside, fingers prodding his nose. A group had gathered around him: boys asking him if he would get revenge; girls chuckling and pointing. Sterling didn't try to give advice, nor did he ask for an explanation. He treated everyone equally rudely, but he was rarely actually mean, and *never* unfair.

Mr. Sterling slowly massaged the dark smudges under his

eyes. "Adam Grant. It's a disgrace that one of the smallest boys in the class has floored the biggest. And especially a boy as warmhearted as Jake Taylor. I'm sure you understand how disgusted I am."

Adam wasn't sure. He thought there was a compliment tangled up in Mr. Sterling's reprimand, and maybe the whole thing was sarcastic. It was always hard to tell with Sterling. Though what he said next was very clear:

"You're suspended. Until Monday."

Adam nodded and looked down.

Mr. Sterling leaned forward and spoke only slightly above a whisper. "Don't get caught being so rash again."

Adam certainly heard an emphasis on the words *get caught*.

And that was it. Mr. Sterling strode off. Adam had two days off school.

Megan's garden was back to back with Adam's, separated only by bushes and a rarely used path that ran between the houses.

They had been friends since before they could remember, and people often joked about how they were like an old married couple. Adam had never previously thought about Megan like that, though recently he had begun to notice things about her that made him uncomfortable. Like how her hair fell against her cheek, and how her swimsuit clung to her. This was the one subject he couldn't talk to Megan about, and he pushed it to a corner of his mind.

That evening Megan appeared through the bushes that separated the gardens.

"He's grounded," said Adam's adopted dad, who was putting away the mower. "He hit a boy at school and has been suspended."

Megan knew: she was in the same class, after all. "Please, Mr. Grant, can I see him for a second?"

Adam's dad sighed. "Okay. But not for long."

Megan dashed in and ran up the stairs. She didn't knock.

Adam lay on his bed in his usual blue shorts and tatty T-shirt, tapping a drumstick on his forehead.

Megan went to the window and half-sat on the ledge. "You *are* stupid. Jake says that he's going to get you," she said.

"And hello to you," Adam said, sitting up. "Look, Meg, I couldn't help it. Leo never does anyone any harm. And Jake is a—prat." He wanted to say something worse, but Megan rarely swore.

Adam wanted to explain that Jake had also been looking at her, but he couldn't find the words to explain it in a way that didn't hint at jealousy.

"I have to write a letter—can you believe it? To Jake! Screw that. I'd rather be expelled."

Megan turned and looked out of the window. "Just write the letter. We all know it doesn't mean anything. You know teachers have to make it look like *something's* being done." She glanced unthinkingly at the bushes at the bottom of the garden. "Come on, we can write it tog—"

She stopped. Then her words came out very slowly and deliberately. "There's someone at the bottom of the garden, in the bushes by the path. He's looking up here."

Adam tapped the drumstick from knee to knee. "Oh, it's probably that lunatic from two doors down looking for his cat again."

"No, Adam. He looks much younger. And this guy's trying not to be seen. He's by that old milk crate."

By the time Adam reached the window the hooded figure had gone, but it was not the first time the house had been watched. Nor would it be the last.

4

Darkness lurked in the tunnel, pressing against the walls, searching for glimmers of light to choke.

A faint rattling came from the rails, then a high-pitched whine echoed closer. The rattle became thunder, the whine a screech. Louder and louder—a mechanical thunder of wheels and carriages. A tube train was on its way.

Nick stood near the exit from the tunnel, backpack hung over one shoulder, school tie short and wide, pants low enough to reveal the red Hugo Boss brand on his boxers. He stood in the same place every morning, trying to get a seat in the last car. His mind was fuzzy with the early-morning thoughts of a boy who was three months shy of his fourteenth birthday.

Rats scampered away from the oncoming train, trampling over one another to hide from the wall of metal that swept away the darkness and replaced it with a blaze of lit cars.

Wires dangled from Nick's ears. "Hurry up," he said into the space over the track. "Come on."

The train hurtled toward the station: a twenty-five miles-per-hour wall of metal.

On the platform a hundred people stood in near silence. Arrivals came every two minutes, announced by a breeze from the tunnel as air was pushed ahead of the train.

A city banker stood to the left of Nick. She did not know that she should have been looking carefully at what was happening around her. But the mornings were always the same: drowsy people heading to work, iPods and iPads, scruffy kids, free newspapers. It was just another day.

The train raced closer, its rumble becoming a rattle, its light just visible on the walls at the bend in the tunnel before the station.

To Nick's right was a girl, slightly older than him, perhaps fifteen. She had dark brown hair and blue eyes. Not ordinary eyes; deep oceans of eyes. He admired the scatter of freckles on her nose.

Nick pulled out his phone to have an excuse to glance down and to the right. She wore white sneakers with no socks. He noticed smooth legs and a short black skirt. She was more than pretty—she looked as if she knew things. Things he wanted to know.

"Hi," he said, glancing away for a second.

"Hello," she mouthed, the sound hidden by the approaching train. Nick only saw the movement of her tongue and lips.

Behind Nick were a man in a suit and a blond boy of about sixteen. The man carried a leather-bound book; the boy's hands hung idly at his side. Like everyone else on the platform they gazed ahead, staring at the tunnel wall and sometimes the adverts. They glanced at the arrivals board that now warned, STAND BACK. TRAIN APPROACHING.

No one thought of murder, or of blood.

The train thundered closer and closer, a fist of metal and air and noise. It sped out of the tunnel, the driver only half aware of his actions as he prepared to slow.

The man shuffled to Nick's left, next to the city banker, and the girl moved a little closer on his right. Nick felt his stomach flip pleasantly as she brushed against him. The boy, arms still limp, had stepped forward to stand immediately behind Nick, who, in the excitement and confusion of girl and train, knew nothing.

The boy pushed out his arms, and Nick was sent into the air over the track. The space was immediately filled with the train.

The driver saw a shape and heard the crack of his window before he understood that the blur was a body. There was a screech of brakes, then several seconds of slowly spinning silence.

Next came screaming and crying. People turned away, united in shock, too late to help. Not that Nick could be helped.

Blood dripped onto a crisp packet that lay between the tracks.

In the confusion, a man in a smart suit, a boy with blond hair and a pretty girl in a short black skirt left the station— unhurried, calm and professional. They had been watching Nick for a long time.

He was the eleventh boy to be killed by The People.

5

Adam awoke. A memory of Jake clutching his bleeding nose jumped into his head. He felt depressed and dragged his covers over his head. Then he leaned across, pulled back the curtains and looked toward Megan's house. Her bedroom faced his, although they were some distance apart. No sign of her this morning. But, he realized, with a pair of binoculars he could probably see in.

"Adam, get dressed. I can hear you're awake." It was his mum.

He went down for breakfast. The good news was that he was allowed out with Megan that afternoon.

Before that, there were jobs as a punishment.

First his dad: "Adam—it hasn't rained for nearly two weeks...."

So he had to water the garden. He actually enjoyed this, as the hose didn't reach the far end, which meant sending a snake of water over improbable distances. He held the hose between his legs and said, "Champion pisser—look, no hands!" until vigorous banging on the window behind him made him stop.

Then his mum: "The washing machine has finished its second load...."

So he had to put clothes on the line. It was boring and fiddly, but the sun was out and he could hear the radio playing some good tunes through the open patio door.

Then Megan appeared through the bushes at the bottom of the garden. She ran up the garden and stood in front of Adam's parents with her hands behind her back, looking completely innocent, more like she was eight years old than just turned fourteen.

"Hello, Mr. Grant. Hello, Mrs. Grant. Is it still okay if we go to Paradise Fields?"

After they left the house, their conversation was mostly about the fight:

"I bet he won't try to hassle *me* again."

"I bet he'll try to *kill* you."

And a few other things:

"I *will* admit to liking Cheryl Cole. *Everyone* does, Meg!"

"Adam, even *you* can tell that new guy on *X Factor* is *way* fitter than Harry Styles!"

Adam was his usual lively self, turning toward Megan and smiling, his arms waving around as if he was a puppet with a drunken operator.

Lost in conversation, they didn't really notice the scruffy teenager on the bench at the corner. He was part of the scenery, like a tree or a passing car. Adam was looking ahead, wondering if Asa would be outside Spar as he had promised.

So they did not notice the boy hiding his stained hoodie behind the bench and following them, at a distance of about a hundred yards, all the way to the shops.

Mr. Rawley's Corner Shop had the best collection of sweets in the area, and was regularly targeted by kids, who nicked their favorites when Mr. Rawley wasn't looking—even Adam had taken a handful on a couple of occasions, though he'd felt guilty both times.

Adam and Megan went in with Asa, who was bragging about his performance on Call of Duty and FIFA and trying to explain to Adam how to get around Internet filters. Megan was more interested in finding the type of licorice that went around in swirls. While they chatted, the bell jangled and in walked the boy from the bench; he went to an aisle near the back, where he put small items in a basket. Unnoticed.

Megan didn't recognize him as the person who had been in the bushes. Equally, he was uninterested in her—or only *indirectly* interested. Asa was of little consequence to him. It was Adam he watched, even as they left the shop and walked up the street.

As soon as they reached the park, mouths full of sweets, Leo came running over. "Jake's here and he wants a scrap. He says that only girls sneak up on people in a fight."

Megan sighed.

Leo continued, voice like a tolling bell, shaking his head slowly. "I don't think you can get out of this."

In the middle of the park was a field, and in the middle of the field was Jake, with three of his mates.

Adam swore. After a brief pause, he said, "Stay here, Meg. I can't avoid him forever."

Insults and swearing drifted across the park toward Adam. Adam couldn't make it all out, but "orphan" and "complete knob" were certainly near the end.

Megan put her hand on Adam's arm. "He's really not worth it."

He pushed her arm away.

Megan sighed again as Adam strode toward Jake.

Megan, Asa and Leo all wanted to see Adam beat Jake, but it looked like an unequal contest. Adam was six inches shorter and had a smaller frame, though he was all muscle. Still, he threw himself at Jake and grappled bravely for a short while, landing a punch or two. Then the pair fell to the ground and Jake's weight winded Adam. A punch just below Adam's belly button followed. Finally, to make his revenge and dominance clear, Jake pushed Adam's face hard into the ground and held it there.

Adam should have stayed still. Everyone could see that it was over. But anger buzzed in him like a thousand wasps and as soon as he was released he threw himself on Jake again. Jake reeled as the punches came: chest, face, shoulder, ear, then back to face. He couldn't recover; couldn't hit back. Jake retreated to the ground as if looking for somewhere to hide.

His friends looked on, dumb spectators.

Megan yelled for Adam to stop. Leo and Asa bellowed for him to continue.

Adam heard nothing. "Leave me alone. And leave Leo alone," he shouted in Jake's face.

Megan ran to him. She pushed her mouth to his ear. "You've *won*. We can go now."

Asa and Leo patted Adam on the back, full of admiration. "Sick," said one; "wow," said the other.

Jake never bothered Adam or Leo again. Nor did anyone else at school. "He beat up Jake Taylor," they said. "He's hard." But the kids at Gospel Oak Senior were not the real threat.

In the corner of the park, between the swings and the roundabout, a seventeen-year-old boy watched Adam intently, wondering when he should make his move.

6

Somewhere in the distance a gate swung lazily against a post. Trees rustled, hushing the night. Drizzle hung in the air. And a car, with little more than a rumble, crept along the quiet residential street, then stopped.

Watery yellow light drifted from the street lamps, and a few early autumn leaves pirouetted to the ground. Otherwise, nothing happened and no one moved.

After a while, a man, a blond-haired boy and a pretty girl stepped out of the car. All three of them were dressed entirely in black. The man carried a leather book.

They had come to kill.

Inside the house, a boy slept soundly, head deep in his pillow, surrounded by posters of soccer players, graffiti art and girl bands. On the floor, next to a crumpled and poorly completed math book, were a PlayStation and a belt. A green light winked from the laptop perched on the end of his bed.

In the distance was the low rumble of a bus pulling away. Here, at 2:00 a.m., everyone slept.

The three strangers didn't enter by the gate: gates creaked. Neither did they enter by the front door: front doors were usually double locked and people recognized their sound. Through oily darkness, they went down the side of the house. Their first five paces were on the left of the path—avoiding recycling boxes and bins. Their next three steps were on the right—stepping around an old fence panel. They had rehearsed this many times. Back at the Old School House everything had been taped out in the gym.

They tiptoed to the patio door at the back of the house. From his top pocket, the man with the book pulled out a small bronze key. Even in the gloom, it went into the lock first time—that had also been practiced on an identical patio door in the gym. They knew it would work: it had been stolen the day before when Marcia had lied about coming to read the electricity meter.

They dared not get this wrong. The four who had failed to kill the boy near Wembley Stadium two months previously had spent fifty-two hours in Dorm Thirteen.

Thoughts of Dorm Thirteen crept into their minds and scuttled around for a moment.

Upstairs, the boy slept.

His parents slept.

They passed through the sitting room and paused briefly at the bottom of the stairs. Items were sometimes left unexpectedly on stairs: toys, clothes, Legos, school bags. But these stairs were clear.

The three went up, all moving in the same way. Right foot first. The fifth and eighth stairs were missed—they creaked. Marcia had discovered this when she had asked to visit the bathroom.

At the top, they headed to the room at the end of the corridor. The girl walked five paces in, then switched on the dim bedside light. The boy woke suddenly, breathing in short bursts.

Initially terrified, the boy slightly relaxed into confusion when he saw a vaguely familiar and very pretty face.

"What's going on? Who...? Why are you...?" he asked blearily.

"Don't worry. Keep quiet and you'll be fine." Deep blue eyes suggested reassurance. "I need to ask you to do something."

She held out a handkerchief.

The boy frowned.

Then she pressed it to his nose and mouth. Initially he took a breath, but sudden dizziness told him that something bad was happening. *This is wrong,* he thought. *Why is she here? Help. HELP.*

HELP ME.

He struggled but the girl's grip was too strong. Her right hand was a vice on his face; her left arm stopped him from rising above the covers.

He began to feel tired and then wanting the oblivion of sleep. It was as if his mind was closing in, shrinking, eaten by darkness. Finally the last glimmer of consciousness in the middle of his head faded.

The other two entered the room.

The man pulled out a syringe and gently inserted the needle into the unconscious boy's arm. A mixture of painkillers, ground-up sleeping pills and illegal drugs poured into him. Like dye dropped into a glass of clear water, the potion unfolded through his body. It reached his heart and billowed out into his arms and legs. It seeped into his brain. His breathing and pulse slowed. Then his body went into spasm and seizure.

His heart stopped.

He died.

Pills and syringes were left on the bedside table.

His parents slept on as the three left the house in silence.

An overdose, it was thought, probably accidental. "The young boy had been experimenting with a variety of drugs," said the police. "Terrifyingly common these days."

But there was one unusual thing about the boy: he had been born at exactly the stroke of midnight at the turn of the millennium, over thirteen years ago.

And he was the twelfth boy to be killed by The People. Twelfth on a list of thirteen.

7

FRIDAY, SEPTEMBER 27, 2013

After Adam had fought Jake in the park, he was treated with a new respect.

One day as he was walking to registration with Megan and Leo, a couple of sixth-form girls came up to him. One, who had the top three buttons of her shirt undone and a skirt barely six inches long, stood behind Adam and put her hands on his shoulders.

"There are real muscles here. Why don't you bring these to me in a couple of years?"

The other pointed at him with a long finger capped by a maroon nail. "You're a wild man, I hear. I hope I don't bump into you while walking home on a dark night." She winked with a knowing look in her eye.

Adam tried to make his brown eyes twinkle.

Mr. Sterling appeared. "Come along, ladies, leave the lad alone."

Megan shook her head slightly. She *really* did not like those girls; the more Adam did, the more she didn't.

Conversation at school was only about two things. One was a headline about the ugly coincidence that a handful of London boys born at the turn of the century had committed suicide. One boy had already been in the papers years before as "the first baby of the millennium." No one in Adam's year had such a birthday, but Leo had been born on the *second* of January, and Asa thought he should be on suicide watch just in case. There was also rapidly increasing discussion and banter about Rock Harvest. This was the last big festival of the year, and brought music fans together for one last gathering before the weather sent everyone indoors. Adam and Megan had been to the festival for the first time the year before. Rachel Meyer, Megan's friend, would also be there, much to the delight of both Asa and Leo, who made no secret of the fact that they fancied her.

"Great line-up, guys," said Asa, who was thought to be an expert on music, at least by himself. "The Stone Roses *and* the Arctic Monkeys *and* the Killers. I hope it doesn't rain as usual."

It was at this point that the boy who swept the playground in the afternoon passed and glanced at Adam. He was the latest in a long line of scruffy characters employed, it seemed, to very slowly redistribute rubbish and leaves, occasionally picking something up. There was, of course, no reason why Adam should have spotted the same boy at the bus stop, in Mr. Rawley's Corner Shop, or reading a magazine on the bench outside Spar. But if Adam had pieced together the jigsaw pieces scattered in his mind, he would have known he had seen him five or six times before.

One event of great significance occurred later the same day. It would never have happened if Adam's bedside clock had not run low on power. Adam had never been good at getting to sleep, but he did like to sleep in and relied on his alarm to be up in time for school.

He sat up in bed in only his pajama bottoms, curtains open in case Megan had *her* binoculars out, and read a magazine. He was halfway through an article on snowboarding when he saw the battery symbol on his alarm clock flashing. He groaned, clicked open the back and saw that he needed two AAA batteries.

His desk drawer held many things: string, elastic bands, half a ruler, a picture from the paper of Megan Fox (why had he kept that? He could Google her), a memory stick that he thought he had lost...Plenty of things, but no batteries.

He padded downstairs, annoyed that his parents were out.

Afterwards, it seemed as if an unseen hand had guided Adam over to the desk in the sitting room, then toward the top right drawer, and then to what lay under the blue folder.

It was a report on Adam's adoption, and raised questions that he had only ever half-asked or been half-told.

Name: *Adam Thomas Grant*

Date of birth: *March 13, 2000*

Date of adoption: *March 13, 2003*

It mentioned a review "because of the exceptional circumstances of the child's adoption," whatever that meant. The 2003 date appeared several times in the writing that followed.

Adam had always known that he was adopted and assumed that had been from birth, or soon after. But he had been three! Adam felt faint and hollow. And his birthday was the same date as his adoption. Very odd. He tore into the desk, looking for more information. He pulled out whole drawers and tipped them onto the floor. Nothing.

Exceptional circumstances? What the hell did that mean? He had been told his mother had died.

He went into his parents' room and looked above the wardrobe. In films and books, things were always hidden there.

Nothing.

Under the bed?

Nothing.

Adam then went from room to room, searching.

By the time his parents returned, the house was a sea of paper. Adam was crouched on the sitting-room floor, still in his pajama bottoms, a letter in his hand.

"When were you going to tell me? I was three—THREE—

when you adopted me! And what does this *exceptional* mean?" Adam jabbed at the page.

His parents looked at one another and his dad—his adopted dad—put his arm around his mum's—his adopted mum's—shoulder. They knew that it was time for the truth to come out.

His mum spoke first, "Oh, Adam, you know how much we love you."

Adam felt his chin crease. No, he didn't want to cry. His eyes leaked, blurring his view.

"Adam, you have been everything we wanted in a son. We could not love you more if you were our own flesh and blood."

Adam choked out his words. "I know that. I know *all* that. But I want to know where I came from. Who I am."

His parents sat on the floor next to him.

Now it was his dad's voice. "We just don't know, Adam. But to us you have been a gift."

"*Please* tell me," said Adam.

Things unsaid for ten years were explained in seconds.

His mum looked straight into his eyes. "You were found in a lady's house. She was sixty-something and couldn't have been your mum. Tests showed that she wasn't related to you at all. And no one knew that you were there. She hadn't formally adopted you. It's like you just landed with her, just like you were given to us. All we do know is that she called you Adam—it was painted on your cot and written on papers in the house—so we kept your name."

"So you don't know where I'm from or when I was born?"

Adam's mum and dad shook their heads. They did not know that Adam was a millennium baby; they did not know that his death was being planned.

They did not know the strange truth that others had worked out.

For Kylie had placed Adam on the steps of what she thought

was a hospital. *His name is ADAM* on an old lottery ticket inside his shirt.

But it was not a hospital. The sign had advertized something very different.

A white background. Bold red writing.

Big Prize BINGO. Tonight!

The lights were bare bulbs, bright and ugly. It was the old movie theater, limping on as a bingo hall.

The cleaner, Mrs. Gowing, had picked Adam up off the steps. She loved him and could not bear to give him away; so, without telling anyone, she had taken him to her home just outside London, in Luton. Despite being called Mrs., she had never married—and though her desire for a husband had passed, her yearning for a child had not.

She cared for Adam until, exhausted from a life of chores and toil, she died sitting in her chair and the postman heard a crying child.

8

Just over a mile away from the Old School House, a couple was walking their dog along a footpath. Unknown to them, they were being observed by a hidden camera.

"What's in there?" asked the woman.

The man peered to see how far ahead their dog had run.

"Not sure. A stately home of some sort?"

As they returned along the main road, a red van pulled in. The words *Royal Mail* could be seen under a thin layer of dust. Leaving the engine running, a woman stepped out with a bundle of packages and letters under her arm. She pressed a buzzer on the gatepost. Before she could turn around, a man in a suit appeared. She wasn't sure where he had come from, but she smiled at him.

"Hello there. More post for the big house?"

"Yes," she replied, pleased that these rich folk had security guards to take parcels to their door. "Not much—just a couple of packages and some letters. This one has come all the way from Vietnam."

"Thanks, love. I'll take them up to Mr. Masters."

With a wave, the postwoman drove off.

The security guard said three numbers into his walkie-talkie, then handed the delivery over to his fellow guard.

He stood on top of a manhole, a circular one just like tens of others across the estate. Underneath the cover was a shallow pit. And in the pit was a heavy cloth bag, with string attaching it to the surface. Inside the bag was a Heckler & Koch submachine gun, a Colt automatic rifle and eight live grenades.

The security guard also had a Browning handgun taped to his lower back, even when he had spoken to the postwoman.

The Old School House was a very different world from the one most people know.

Viper waited in silence for her history lesson to begin. Her essay, 1,200 words in neat handwriting on the subject of the Demon of Poitiers, sat on her desk. She could hear fragments of a geography lesson through the wall: "The Transylvanian Mountains will be important when the Reign comes. The inhabitants will be resettled and the entire area will be used by The People."

Mr. Webb tapped his stick on the desk and the class stood. They chanted together: "The Master is watching; Lord Coron is watching; to serve one is to please the other." Lessons always began in the same way.

"Today I've been instructed to say a few words about how close we are to the Reign of The People."

They all knew the basics:

First, the Imposter would come. The first man, Adam, was created in 4000 BC; Abraham revealed the Law in 2000 BC; the old god used the man Jesus 2,000 years after that; and in AD 2000 the Imposter was born. It was elegantly simple maths. Events exactly 2,000 years apart to the day.

Next would come the Reign of The People. They all knew their thousand-year rule would begin when the Imposter, Adam, was killed.

The world would turn to Lord Coron and The People, who would reign for 1,000 years. Lord Coron—visionary, leader, healer—would guide events.

Everyone knew this. It was obvious. You had to be evil or stupid to deny it.

They all knew that only one person could stop this glorious reign.

The Imposter.

A boy born at the center of world business and trade to a single mother.

A boy who united everyone in hatred.

A boy they had to find.

A boy hated even more than the Traitor—the one person to leave The People and live.

Both had to die. They all knew that.

And of the thirteen possible Imposter candidates, twelve were now dead.

Mr. Webb said, "The beginning of the Reign of The People is now very close. The Imposter has been found. He is the one we suspected all along. The one to escape Lord Coron at the moment of his birth."

They all knew the story of Coron's glorious attempt on millennium night to free the world from the Imposter.

Their teacher continued: "The Blessed will be sent."

And they all knew what that meant: the Blessed. Those who were special, raised above the rules that smothered ordinary people. Blessed killers.

Viper hoped that she would be one of them again. She and Cobra. Twice before they had gone with Coron himself. But this was the vital one. The Imposter. For real.

Please, please, let it be me, she thought.

Outside, some children played a game that looked, from a distance, like rugby. But there was no ball. In this game, both sides tried to push a neutral person, called the runner, over their opponent's goal line.

No one knew of rugby, or soccer or cricket. Most of the

children didn't know of television, or had forgotten. There were no newspapers. No books from outside. Almost everyone under eight or nine had never gone beyond the fences.

The runner looked as if he was going to win the game of Mandown. It was rare for the runner to win, even rarer for him or her to escape unhurt, but Python was fast.

In the geography lesson, Mamba glanced out of the window, idly watching the game of Mandown being played out on the pitch. Suddenly a stick whacked down on his left hand. A stinging line of red ran like an angry river just above his knuckles.

"Mamba isn't concentrating. Again." Mr. Sansom pointed with his stick to Mamba's right hand until it was laid flat on the desk.

Whack!

Everyone knew there would be more to come.

"You have been warned about this."

Mamba hoped the punishment would be short.

"As you seem fascinated by the Mandown game being played outside, you can be the runner in this evening's game."

Mamba looked down. "Yes, my teacher." Evening games were played by the oldest kids and sometimes some of the adults. The runner was certain to be injured.

But the punishment was not over.

Mr. Sansom's stick pointed from boy to girl around the classroom. Finally, it stopped on Boa, a small and blemished girl. Though she had been born in the Old School House, she had never been popular.

"Boa—you will share in the punishment."

The rules were simple. To show that wrongdoing weakened the community, and to encourage the group to correct its own faults, someone else shared in the punishment. Boa had been chosen.

"Boa will not eat until sundown tomorrow."

Mamba was relieved. It could have been worse. He knew he must work harder to serve his master. To serve Coron. He rubbed his stinging hand and resolved to do better.

9

Not knowing where Adam was tormented and agonized Coron. It corroded him.

Adam. Adam. Adam. Adam.

The name bubbled in his mind hour after hour after hour. Where *was* he?

Coron's mind was welded straight, unbending, like railway tracks heading into the murky distance. Though others born at that moment had been killed, their deaths left Coron unfulfilled. He had to kill *Adam*—the boy who had escaped him on millennium night.

Adam. Adam. Adam. Adam.

Then, late one evening, someone researching at the Old School House found the story of a woman who had died and had been discovered with a baby boy who wasn't hers. And he was called *Adam.*

It led to one of the 5,400 adoptions in 2003. Why had they wasted so long investigating the previous year's cases?

For this mistake, people suffered.

Adam. Adam. Adam. Adam.

Adopted by Mr. and Mrs. Grant.

Grant. Adam. Adam Grant. Could it be?

Yes.

*   *   *

Most days come and go and are forgotten, lost in the patchy smog that is the past. But every now and again one rises above this drifting haze, and Wednesday, October 16, was such a day for Adam and Megan.

After school, Adam was crossing the playground with Asa, who was delivering another lecture on Call of Duty and whether it really would be best to kill zombies with a Colt M1911, when a group of year sevens having a kick-about knocked a ball into his path. Adam was as good as anyone in year nine at football, so when the ball came toward him, he sent it like a comet back across the playground.

There was a dreadful inevitability about what happened next.

Emerging from the shed-like classroom, known to all as the Mobile, was Madame Dubois, the French teacher. She was talking to Megan's friend, Rachel Meyer, a girl adored by teachers almost as much as by boys, despite having a tendency to slack off.

Madame Dubois seemed determined to stand at exactly the point where the ball was going to land. It flew through the air and hit her square on the forehead, then ricocheted into the nearest pane of glass.

"You couldn't do that again if you tried," said Asa. "What a strike!"

"Oh no," mumbled Adam. The year sevens were looking on in admiration: to do this *and* beat up Jake Taylor—well, that made Adam Grant a hero, almost a god.

"Why can't you keep your bloody ball to yourself?" Adam said to his admirers, who loved that he swore despite the arrival of Mr. Sterling, though Adam had not seen him striding over.

"Adam Grant," the deputy head muttered, slightly indistinctly, "you will assist with the cleanup operation and apologize to Madame Dubois." He then added, after a pause, "Your *latest* victim."

Asa had run over to check on the wellbeing of Rachel Meyer and, in passing, Madame Dubois.

Megan insisted on staying while Adam helped carry the boards to cover the hole. Asa left carrying Rachel's bag and chuckling at everything she said. Madame Dubois retreated to the staff room and drank peppermint tea.

The boy who swept the playground came over with a hammer and nails. He avoided eye contact. The kids tended to sneer at such characters.

As he stretched to hold the wood in place, Megan noticed a deep scar, about as long as her hand, on the boy's neck. But this thought was tangled up with so many others. In any case, this boy looked rough, the sort of person Megan's parents warned her to keep away from.

Eventually Adam and Megan wandered off, the last to leave school.

"Come on," said Megan. "Let's go home the long way, past the kiosk in the park. We've got half an hour, and I kept a fiver from the weekend."

It was this decision that proved to be the most important of the afternoon.

Adam and Megan sat on one of the picnic tables behind the kiosk. Megan was looking at Adam. She *really* liked the way he was still slightly sunburned on his nose, though she didn't understand why that appealed. They chatted about Asa and Rachel, but were thinking about themselves.

"Don't say anything to anyone, but she thinks that boy in year eleven is really fit. You know, the swimmer."

Adam was so absorbed in Megan and her conversation that he didn't consider jealousy. "Yes. He's pretty hench, I suppose. But Asa really fancies Rachel."

Looking over Adam's shoulder for an instant, Megan saw something that made her frown. Two or three trees back, half hidden, someone was watching them. Then a parade of images came at her like photographs falling from an album: the guy by the bushes, the boy on the bench, the young man in the shop. The cleaner at school! And the person looking at them now. They were one and the same. Other indistinct pictures and vague outlines were also scattered in the corners of her mind.

She went pale and looked down. "Adam, I've noticed something."

Adam wiped his face, fearing a booger. But Megan wasn't joking around.

"Adam, we're being watched, and have been for some time. It's the guy from school, you know, the one that sweeps the playground. How creepy!"

Adam knew Megan well enough to realize she wasn't messing about, so he didn't argue or ask for an explanation. He trusted her completely. "Okay, let's go. It's getting late anyway." But he couldn't resist glancing around.

And that was when the older boy decided to make his move.

As Adam and Megan scurried across the field toward the ponds and the gate beyond, the boy dashed along the path, quickly overtaking dog walkers, parents with strollers and occasional clusters of kids. One or two people tutted and glared as he pushed past, but all seemed to think that he was someone best left alone.

Adam and Megan broke into a run. "This is stupid," Megan panted. "Why don't we get someone to help?"

But at this point, by the first pond, everyone seemed to have melted away.

In his black tracksuit, the boy looked threatening, exactly like the sort of person Adam and Megan had heard stories about. Young enough to want to beat them up, but old enough to . . . They didn't like to think about it. "Come *on*," Megan said, tugging on Adam's arm.

Adam had stopped momentarily, thinking he would stay and fight—mainly to impress Megan—but anger had not mastered his fear. The boy after them had the build of a man. And he was getting closer. So Adam followed Megan along the curved path between the trees and ponds, away from the gate, heading for a hole in the fence that came out onto Park Avenue, opposite the Green Dragon pub. They would never get there before the boy caught up. Adam reached out to stop her. "Meg, he'll get to us."

Megan stepped into the pond and started wading across. The water only came up to their thighs, and it made the route to the exit much, much shorter. As they stepped out on the far side and dashed between the bushes beyond, their pursuer arrived on the path, barely fifteen yards away. If they had been just a bit faster, he might never have seen them slip away. But he did, and he also waded in. "Stop!" he shouted.

On the other side of the pond, Adam and Megan darted through the bushes. Older kids sometimes used this area, and debris littered the undergrowth: cigarette ends, a bottle, some cans, plastic bags.

Suddenly, they reached the gap in the fence and the bright late-afternoon sunlight of Park Avenue beyond. And there, a huge red savior, with doors open and a driver telling them, "Now 'urry up if you're gonna get on"—the number thirteen bus.

Perfect.

They leaped on, hearts thumping with the euphoria of escape. They swiped bus passes, the doors closed, and the bus quickly pulled away.

The older boy stumbled onto the street, looked left and right, and sank to his knees.

On the bus, Adam and Megan sat downstairs at the back, trousers and skirt dripping wet, shoes squelching. Bubbles of water appeared on the floor as Adam pushed his feet down. They talked, half reflecting on the action, half considering what they would do and who they would tell.

Then Adam, still annoyed that he had not been braver and dealt with this character in the same way he had dealt with Jake

Taylor, did something that required equal nerve. He put his left arm around Megan's shoulder. He wouldn't have done it normally, of course, but the excitement made him irrational.

Megan didn't pull away. She turned her head toward Adam.

His chest felt full of electricity, and tight, like china about to crack. He pushed his lips to Megan's—just for a second, perhaps two—until the bus pulled up with a slight jolt. It had arrived at their stop.

10

THURSDAY, OCTOBER 17, 2013

Coron stood before the assembly. Almost one hundred people sat before him: women to the left, men to the right and children in the center. The People.

Coron rarely shouted. His voice was soft, even gentle, like a calming stream. But when he did shout he was thunder and excitement. It wasn't what Coron said that drew people in, nor even how he said it—it was Coron himself. He knew. He knew the past and the future; he read thoughts and understood emotions; he explained doubts and soothed fears; his approval inspired; his anger destroyed.

To be alongside him was to share in glory and victory.

Many had joined The People, especially in the early days, because they had heard Coron speak. He stood on corners and spoke to shoppers. He sidled up to lonely individuals in bus stations and tearooms. He also visited the meetings of extreme political groups, a pool which had spawned some important members.

But, increasingly, recruits were children. Some were the sons and daughters of members. Others had been taken from the streets: young runaways, mistreated girls, neglected and beaten boys—those who wanted something new and safe. A routine. Discipline. The younger the better, Coron said to those who went out to fish for new members. Adults are dangerous, corrupted, their motives and desires twisted like old tree roots. Children—those thirteen years and younger—are much better: innocent, teachable, spirited.

Once a week Coron addressed all of The People. He never prepared, never used notes. He spoke as the Master instructed him.

"The Master's work in heaven is almost complete. He directed his righteous army of angels against the deceiver who sat on the throne. The old god has been defeated; the New God, the Master, is about to take his place. And what has happened in heaven is about to be repeated on earth.

"People in the world are like stones, unaware of what is happening, lying in the mud, senseless and stupid. They don't live as we do; their lives are worth no more than rough soil. They are slaves, shuffling from work to sleep, trapped in a machine that dulls and controls. I have seen them, drifting around the streets, drugged by dull television and confused music. Not us—we are free servants of a glorious master! We are taught and guided—we are unique. We are alive!

"To be alone in the world is to be an angry infant: unsettled, untrained, uncomfortable. To be one of The People is to be special, rewarded and free.

"Yes, we are trained, led by a fair and righteous master. We are to be kings! Yes, you will rule, and you will be honored, needed... loved.

"And that time is very near. Yes, I tell you now: our rule will begin at the moment that the Imposter is dead. Soon we will leave here and take our rightful place.

"We are the only people who are truly alive!"

Those who listened to Coron sat in silent excitement, thrilled by their knowledge and its contrast with the blind world outside.

Later, in the cellar that had become a dark chapel, Coron held his arms at right angles so that his raised cloak looked like black wings. His palms were outstretched, revealing deep, neat scars. His eyes were closed and a mumble came from his fast-moving lips.

Then he spoke clearly: "I beg to hear your instructions, Master."

The room was in near-darkness, lit only by thirteen large candles. Two figures knelt on either side of Coron; they were also dressed in black and had closed eyes. In front of them was a stone table—an altar—with a leather-bound book in the middle.

Coron repeated himself: "I beg to hear your instructions, Master."

Coron squinted and saw burning pebble eyes slowly melt out of the gloom, then a wrinkled face, deeply lined like an old man's, then hair, in long tufts, and then a thin, bony body almost covered by a cloak.

Coron did not pretend this. Yet no spirit stood in front of him. The demon was a shadowy production, a sort of echo, of Coron's sick mind. Madness is imaginative—far more so than sanity.

"Master, we have done your will. Only Adam remains."

The vision roared. "HE MUST DIE! The Imposter still prevents us taking our place of honor. You must burn him off the page. This boy must die before he comes of age."

Before he comes of age. Before he turns fourteen.

Most people keep their darkest thoughts in locked vaults, but Coron's mind was a castle with open doors. He explored his madness and searched in its corners for bony scraps of evil to gnaw on.

The vision spoke again: "Death must embrace the Imposter."

"Master. What else?"

"Time is now short, and still the work is undone. Those who have failed must be punished properly."

Coron's mind danced to Dorm Thirteen. The place of punishment. His thoughts, though unformed, shrieked at him.

"Yes. Yes."

A heavy door opened behind Coron and a whimpering could be heard.

Coron did not need to turn round. "Master," he said, "we have something to offer you."

11

On Thursday, October 17, Adam and his parents sat in front of the headmistress, Mrs. Tavistock.

"Mr. and Mrs. Grant, I can assure you that this young man went through all the usual checks, and if he turns up at school I will ask him to explain himself," she said in a high-pitched voice.

The trombone-like tones of Mr. Sterling broke in. "We won't see him today." A gray haze of whiskers covered his pale, slightly sagging skin. His shirt had not been ironed.

Mrs. Tavistock continued primly, "If he *does* turn up, he will have some serious questions to answer."

"He won't turn up." It was Mr. Sterling again. "I went to his address on the way here."

"You didn't mention that, Rob, um, Mr. Sterling," Mrs. Tavistock said, smiling rather too enthusiastically. "I think we should talk about this."

Like a crowd at a tennis match, Adam and his parents looked from Mr. Sterling to Mrs. Tavistock.

Mr. Sterling shifted in his chair and shrugged slightly. "The flat he claimed to have moved to doesn't exist. There's no number thirteen in the block at all. No *Barry Crow* in any of the eight flats. I asked. And the address he gave when we first did the checks now has a Chinese family living in it."

Mrs. Tavistock continued, her voice making recorder sounds that danced around the subject, desperately proving that the school was not at fault, and that—very much in second place—Adam's parents had nothing to worry about.

As they were leaving, Adam's dad turned to Mr. Sterling. "So that's the end of this business, is it?"

Mr. Sterling sniffed. "Maybe."

Adam's mum was getting anxious. She thought she could smell whisky.

"It's strange that he chose that moment to strike," Mr. Sterling added, almost as an afterthought.

"True." Adam, with a frown, spoke for the first time. "Why did he watch us for so long? And why come into our garden?" Everyone in the room shivered a little.

Then Mr. Sterling again, with one final rumble: "Obviously no logic to these nutters."

It was Megan's parents who insisted on visiting the police station. Megan's mother was a lawyer who was often there for one reason or another, and her father did something in the legal department of a bank. The entrance hall was busy with the usual mix of police officers, harassed victims and shifty characters.

Leaning over the front desk, Adam and Megan told the story in full, enjoying the questions and the setting. A policewoman took down every detail and promised to investigate. She clearly thought Mr. Sterling had made a mistake about the flat, but said they would check. All of the adults assumed they were dealing with an unhinged lunatic.

As they turned to leave, another policeman stopped them. He had three stripes on his badge, rather than just letters and numbers, and he introduced himself as a chief inspector. Adam remembered the rank, but missed the man's name.

"Ah. I've heard you are here about the incident in the park," the chief inspector said. "Could you have a look at some mug shots in one of the interview rooms?"

This sounded even more fascinating. All of a sudden Megan and Adam were being taken seriously.

They leaned over a table and were shown some pictures of older teenagers. "No," said Megan, and "No," said Adam, one after another, sometimes together. Adam ensured they had to push their shoulders together to look at the pictures properly.

"What about this boy?" the chief inspector asked. "He has a scar."

"No," said Megan, thinking. "He's similar, but not quite."

It was like an American cop show.

Megan thought, then said, "Scar?"

"Yes," replied the chief inspector.

"How did...?"

"*You* said he had a scar."

In the confusion Megan thought she must have forgotten, and the moment passed. Only later did she realize that she had certainly never mentioned a scar.

The events in the park and the inquiry afterward were soon forgotten. Adam and Megan were walked to and from school for a week and a long assembly on "Stranger Danger" was endured by everyone. But the soap opera that was Rock Harvest rapidly dominated everyone's minds.

The music was only half the interest. Any hint that a boy was actually attending *with a girl* was thought to be headline news.

Asa didn't play down his connection with Rachel. "I wouldn't *exactly* say that she is going with me, but let's just say that we'll be seeing a fair bit of one another. And when I say that I'll be seeing a fair bit of her, I think you know what I mean." His eyebrows danced up and down.

Adam and Leo nudged one another.

Leo, to his deep regret, was not as popular with girls as the other two. He was the only boy in the class who could compete with Megan in exams, but this didn't seem to impress the opposite sex. "I think I'll see what's on offer when I get there," he said, trying to convey bravado.

Leo and Asa turned to Adam.

"I'm not really that interested in girls at the moment," Adam said.

"I knew it," laughed Asa. "You and Megan are together!"

Saturday was the first day of half-term and the start of the festival. Euston Station was full of those heading to the site. Most were in their late teens and early twenties, but there were plenty of younger children accompanied by parents who huddled together like penguins. Scattered among the crowd were the professional festival goers: studs, piercings and dreadlocks marked them out as a distinct tribe. Large green backpacks and rolled-up sleeping bags hung from backs.

Adam and Megan stood with Leo, Asa and Rachel as part of a larger group that was going from their school. Asa's parents had volunteered to accompany them. They had the air of having once been cool, unlike Adam's mum and dad. Jake Taylor and his friends had gone down earlier to "get things started."

The eleven o'clock train was already in the platform when the announcement came. "The train at platform thirteen is the Rock Harvest special..." The rest was lost in a cheer and a rumble as hundreds of feet poured in that direction.

It was standing room only in the cars. In Coach E, Adam was enjoying the opportunity to be very close to Megan, who was writing her initials, M.E.J., in steam on the window. But as Adam's thoughts began to spin faster and faster, Leo's face appeared right next to his.

"Phew, that bog stinks," Leo said. "Someone must have left a turd on the floor."

The train was about to pull away when a boy with a scar

leaped into the last car, Coach M. Those by the door resisted, but he was determined.

"Hold it, mate, we're full in here," said a large Australian.

"I am staying on this train," said the seventeen-year-old, staring fiercely at the Aussie until he turned away.

Also in Coach B was a group of four children. Oddly for their age, they weren't accompanied by an adult. No one noticed; they were just kids going to the festival. Four tickets out of seventy thousand.

They had been told two days before that they were going.

12

In what had once been a grand drawing room, Coron stood in front of children sitting on long wooden benches. Behind them, their arms behind their backs, were three other adults.

"Children, life is full of choices. Sitting still is a choice; running around is a choice. It is a choice to eat potatoes rather than stones. And it is my responsibility to teach you to make the right choice."

Coron beckoned for a girl to come forward.

"Viper has served well. She has done what is right in the eyes of the Master. He told me that she deserves great reward."

Viper stepped forward. She had dark blue eyes and freckles on her nose. Memories of her service—helping in two important deaths—made her proud. Viper knew nothing of life outside The People: her father had been one of Coron's first recruits, and she had grown up in the Old School House.

Coron continued. "Here taking a life would be a terrible thing. But vermin are different. Even we can kill rats."

The children listened obediently.

"Viper has helped to rid the world of two disgusting creatures. And she has been chosen for an even greater task: to kill the remaining and most dangerous *rat*. One that carries *infection* and *disease*."

The girl bit her bottom lip and smiled.

Coron turned to the other side of the room. "Cobra, come here." Cobra's height and athletic figure made him a natural leader among the children. His unusual combination of brown eyes and blond hair were widely admired.

"Cobra will also go and help kill this rat. Cobra, I trust you."

The slightest hint of pleasure passed across Cobra's face.

Coron continued, "Two others will join them. Asp and Python, stand up." One girl and one boy stood. "You also have this exciting honor. But be wary: this rat has razors for claws: they can spring out and cut you open. And his entire body is full of burning poison. I know that you will stamp on him. Stamp on him and bury him in the ground."

All four bowed slightly.

Viper and Cobra returned to their places. Asp and Python sat down.

"But not everyone always makes the right choice. If you put your hand into a wild animal's cage, we would slap you as a warning, to protect you."

He paused.

"Adder, stand up and come here."

A boy of about eleven stepped forward. At age eight he had been found in a shopping center, trying to keep warm, escaping from parents who neglected him. His memories of that time were beginning to fade. He knew that things were better for him, and leaving The People was simply not an option. Only one person had left, and everyone hated him. No one else had gone, though one or two had tried.

"Adder has been to the Far Fence without permission. Not even adults would do such a thing. And you know why we stay away? Because of the *scum* that may grab you and turn your brain into stinking filth." Coron's face was tight and his teeth ground together.

Adder faced the ground.

"So Adder will be punished. One day he may have the honor

of meeting the Master himself, for I can see that Adder has learned much already. But today is a lesson. A punishment."

Coron grabbed a fistful of the boy's hair. "I have decided that he will spend twelve hours in Dorm Thirteen."

The boy considered pleading. His lips moved and he made a ticking sound in the back of his throat. Inside he was screaming.

Three or four dreadful seconds hung in the room. It was unusual for a child to be sent up to Dorm Thirteen.

In the instant before he was going to be sent away, Adder finally spoke in one quick burst. "Please-I-am-sorry-anything-but-that."

Coron looked at Viper and smiled. "Very well."

Viper smiled back. On the other side of the room, Cobra also smiled. He knew exactly what was going to happen next.

"Very well," said Coron. "Twenty-four hours in Dorm Thirteen. And if you speak again it will be two days."

Even adults struggled with two days in Dorm Thirteen. Few could endure three or four days. And those who stayed in Dorm Thirteen for a week always went mad.

Down the corridor in the Old School House was what could have been a police incident room.

Thirteen pictures circled the walls: the thirteen boys who had been born to single parents in London within an hour of the new millennium. Boys who could be the Imposter. Four were recent pictures of thirteen-year-olds; others were of younger boys. The youngest wore short trousers and was holding a yo-yo.

Twelve of the pictures had a neat red line drawn through them.

The thirteenth picture was of the one boy who remained alive: Adam Grant. The one who had escaped on millennium night and then gone missing. The Master had confirmed that he was the one. The Imposter.

Seven people stood in front of a display board. Labeled pictures of Adam and his parents and friends were stapled to it; a schedule of his movements was linked to other material by pins and cord. A recent addition was a floor plan of Adam's house, his bedroom shaded in red. Though neither Adam nor his parents had ever seen his birth certificate, a copy was pinned next to an adoption letter.

Many hundreds of hours of detective work had been invested in this project.

On the right-hand side of the board was information about Rock Harvest. A finger tapped the words The Hill of Sacrifice on a map. "He will be taken here," said a middle-aged woman. "This is where Adam will be killed."

part two

13

THE WEEKEND OF SATURDAY, OCTOBER 26, 2013

From the air Rock Harvest looked like an organized colony of busy insects, but on the ground it had the color and variety of a carnival. Nearly 70,000 people were crammed onto the site midway between London and Birmingham.

After a short burst of activity setting up camp, and experimenting whether it was possible for Adam, Asa *and* Leo to fit into a two-man tent, the group strode off toward the music. Asa's parents ambled away, their cool reputation withering fast.

In front of the main stage, a swarm of people bounced up and down waving their arms. Deep beats thundered from the distant band. Leo was sent out as a probe to see how far forward it was possible to get, but soon returned shaking his head and looking harassed.

Rachel suggested drinks.

"Yeah, what do you want?" said Asa, putting his arm around her shoulder.

Rachel was used to such attention. She used her thumb to pull his jeans down slightly at the back. "It depends what you're offering."

Asa had wanted to get out of his league, but now that he was suddenly there, he was flustered.

"Er, a can of Coke?"

Megan said that there was someone good on the second stage, so they headed there, past short lines for funfair rides and longer ones for bathrooms, not seeing anyone they knew.

Here they could get near the front, just. The group was a new one called Test Tube Kids: they were at the rock end of disco music, ideal for Adam, whose body seemed to have a gymnast's flexibility, Megan noticed. Megan loved the dancing and found the experience thrilling but confusing—the noise, music and lights meant that she couldn't concentrate on any one thing. "Keep away from anything that you don't like the look of," her parents had said. She pushed the warning from her mind.

Rachel was dancing with about five or six boys, including a couple who looked over sixteen. She was remarkable, arching her body back and then moving her shoulders forward, and sometimes resting her hands on boys' shoulders. Asa had to prance around ever more athletically to keep her attention.

Leo's legs and arms did not seem to move with any reference to one another. He looked like an alien whose sucker-pad limbs kept slipping apart. Amused pity from a couple of fifteen-year-old girls was misread by him as genuine interest.

It was then that the band moved their hands above their heads, a circular space opened up and several hundred people started moving in the same anticlockwise direction, round and round.

"Yes!" said Asa. "Mosh pit!"

All five in their group were caught up in the movement, though Megan, Rachel and Leo soon pushed their way to the side, panting heavily and sweating.

"Sick," they agreed, trying to catch sight of the other two.

Adam and Asa were swept along by the excitement and whirlpool movement. They were the youngest there, so older teenagers shouted encouragement, but after a minute or two they wanted to escape. All of a sudden they found it hard to keep their footing and were elbowed once or twice. Then Asa fell. People did try to avoid Adam as he leaned down to help, but momentum carried some into his back. He was nudged forward, then spun away from Asa.

He couldn't get back. It was as if bodies were being sent to knock him down. They came too fast. Nudge. Prod. Bump. Adam let out a string of swear words.

There was a sharper jolt, and Adam tripped and twisted to the ground, trying to grab hold of people around him. A boot scuffed the back of his head, and he raised his hands to shield his face; then a foot jabbed into his ribs; there was a lot of pressure on his upper leg—"Get off me!"—and then he couldn't distinguish the smacks and pokes that came like wasp stings.

"Stop! Help!"

He was wrapped in indistinct loud noises and could see nothing but hundreds of blurred legs. Sooner or later someone was going to stand on his head.

Words tumbled out of him: "Help-me-someone-help-me-now-get-off-help-me-now!"

Then he felt himself being lifted up, firmly; hands were under each shoulder. A couple of dancers had grabbed him, one on either side, and pulled him to safety, which was actually only a few feet away.

"Are you okay?" they asked, leaning toward Adam. They were about fifteen or sixteen. "That was amazing."

"Yeah, thanks, mate," he said, trying to look as if the experience had been expected and entertaining.

Asa arrived, having also been rescued by two slightly older dancers.

Megan, Rachel and Leo ran over. "You should *not* have been in there!" shouted Leo.

"It was brilliant," said Asa.

"Come on," said the oldest rescuer. "Let's get you away from here."

The group, now nine in total, wound their way past those who were still dancing and slumped on the muddy ground next to a popcorn and cotton candy stall.

"I could do with something to eat," said Rachel. She was looking at the oldest boy, who was all blond hair and muscles. She thought he looked like Alex Pettyfer. Rachel, a goddess to most boys, had Alex Pettyfer as her god.

One of the two girls spoke to Adam. "You really should stay out of that stuff until you're a bit older, but you're a sick dancer." Adam was flattered. He looked into the girl's deep blue eyes—eyes the same color as Megan's, but much more grown-up somehow.

"Thanks. Can I buy you all a drink, as a thank-you for getting me out of there?" suggested Adam.

The group ended up spending the rest of Saturday evening together, and by 11:00 p.m. on Saturday it was as if they had all been friends for years. By Sunday evening they were like family.

The action was wilder on Sunday, with everyone trying to make the most of the last evening. There were so many people that although the site was less than a mile from end to end, it was impossible to find anyone else, especially as there was no cell phone reception.

The blond boy was called Keenan, which he said meant "fair-headed" in Irish. The pretty girl was Cassie: "I don't know where that comes from, but it probably means clever and sexy," she said in a way that made Adam and Asa look at one another and Megan roll her eyes. The other two were named Harry and Sofia.

After checking in with Asa's parents at *exactly* the agreed time—a ploy to make sure that they were allowed to stay out until the music stopped at midnight—the group split up. Leo was talked into visiting the DJ tent with the other two newcomers. An exhausted Asa said that he was keen to dance in front of the main stage with Rachel. Harry and Sofia also drifted off. So Adam and Megan were left alone with Keenan and Cassie.

Year eleven seemed an exotic and distant land for Adam and Megan, who were in year nine. Adam had already started to flick his hair back in the same way as Keenan; Megan had a hushed conversation with Cassie about kissing.

Adam and Megan never considered that they were in terrible danger. They thought that Keenan and Cassie were ordinary kids.

They never saw a seventeen-year-old boy with a long scar on his neck watching them.

10:15 p.m.

"How about going on the rides before they close?" said Keenan. "You can still hear the main stage from there."

There were three main rides, none of which had long lines. The Frisbee was certainly the most exciting, but Megan and Cassie weren't keen. "If I puke up there, it'll go on people down here," said Cassie. There was also one called Starship, in which riders were spun around while pressed against a circular wall. But they chose Tornado, the gentlest, which allowed all four of them to go on together.

10:30 p.m.

They whirled and twisted and pressed together, whooping and screaming, dizzy with spinning and laughter. Lights and sound twirled around them. Adam had one arm around Megan—*amazing Megan*—and one arm round Cassie, who was soft to touch and *very* pretty.

He stepped off the ride feeling happier than ever and pulled Megan over, briefly hugging her. "That was great, wasn't it?"

For a second—what a second—she had both arms around him, hugging him back. "Yes, it was."

"How about going back to our tent to chill out?" said Keenan. "Come on, you've got an hour."

10:55 p.m.

The tent was big enough for four. "This is where Harry and I sleep," said Keenan. Harry seemed friendly enough, but he wasn't an imposing and impressive character like Keenan. "Cassie and Sofia are next door." Keenan pulled out a large brown bottle. "How about something to get the party going? Just a swig?"

Megan was not keen. Her parents nearly hadn't let her go to the festival at all. "Don't drink. And stay away from anything that looks like drugs," they had warned her, over and over.

Cassie said that she would have some; Adam also. He felt very daring and several years older than he was. Megan agreed to a drop, which resulted in three-quarters of a plastic cup. They all sat with cider in front of them.

"Come on then," said Keenan. And he drank first. "How about truth or dare?"

Adam and Megan smiled and gave mock groans, then nodded.

11:25 p.m.

This had to be the last go, because all four had spotted the time on Keenan's alarm clock. Adam was determined to go for dare again, hoping that he would have to kiss Megan.

Keenan had a different idea. "You have to run down to the first-aid tent, with your T-shirt off, shouting, 'I love Megan, I love Megan.' "

Adam's disappointment was lessened by the thought that this might still lead to a kiss later. "Okay," he said as he pulled off his top. He quickly leaped outside, bolstered by cider, so not as shy as he would normally have been in front of those returning to their tents.

"I love Megan! I love Megan!"

He jumped over ropes and between tents, even cupping his hands to his mouth, racing all the way there. Done it. He began to head back, still yelling. "I love Megan! I love—"

Then he stopped. Between him and Keenan's tent was the teenager from the park. For a few seconds they faced one another like gunslingers about to draw weapons.

"No!" Adam felt drained and cold inside. He had to get back. Keenan looked tough; he would help.

Unable to head straight there, and struggling to see clearly in the dark, he went down one row, where the path was slightly wider, and sprinted in what he thought was the right direction. He didn't look to either side, just ran with all his strength until he finally spotted the brown and gray of Keenan's tent. Sighing with relief, Adam fell breathlessly inside.

11:35 p.m.
A hand immediately grabbed his throat and he was pushed harshly to the ground. Knees on his back. His legs pinned down.

Then a voice: "Truth or dare?" It was Keenan.

Adam thought of the bloke chasing him, who surely wouldn't be far away. "Stop messing about! There's someone after me."

Adam could hear chuckling. Was that Harry?

"Answer me—truth or dare?"

Adam was suddenly desperate. "Let me go, you bastard."

Keenan, usually called Cobra, grabbed the side of Adam's face and pulled the skin tight. "Truth or dare?" he insisted.

"Truth?" said Adam.

"You're coming with us. Don't make a sound, or your girlfriend will get hurt."

Megan? Where was she? Adam didn't want her hurt. He had no choice. "Okay."

He was hauled upright, Harry on one arm and a girl he hadn't seen before on the other.

Why the hell were they doing this? He had no idea how their game had suddenly become twisted and scary.

"And, just in case you were thinking of shouting for help, you'll find that this really keeps the noise down," said Keenan. He stuffed a handkerchief into Adam's mouth. Though Adam could still breathe, it deadened any sound he tried to make.

"This also keeps the noise down," said Keenan, punching Adam in the face. Unable to move his arms, Adam couldn't stop his eyes from watering.

Keenan picked up a large leather-bound book and put it in a backpack.

Adam was marched out of the tent, then back toward the trees. He knew that fields were beyond: he had seen them when they arrived. Were they going to beat him up? What had he done? Did this have something to do with Jake? Terrified that something would happen to Megan, Adam didn't speak until they were well beyond the tents. Then his voice came out like a low siren through the handkerchief. "Why? Why?"

He was ignored, and step by step the tents disappeared into the distance, until Adam was pushed between a gap in the fence and all was darkness.

They kept walking.

"What's going on? What do you want?" Adam pleaded for answers.

11:50 p.m.

Keenan spoke. "Before you die, I'll tell you what you are. You are filth, but you are dangerous. Born at midnight at the millennium, two thousand years after the previous Imposter, you—"

"I wasn't. I wasn't," Adam tried to say. But he was.

"You would stop Lord Coron, who will cleanse this world, from taking his real place, perhaps with me at his side."

Coron? Cleanse the world? What was Keenan going on about? This was mad!

Adam realized that these people were completely crazy. He was terrified and things didn't make sense. They really were going to kill him! He struggled, throwing his body around, desperately trying to break free. Keenan put a hand on either side of Adam's mouth and pressed in. Then he jabbed him hard with his fist. Adam's world shrank to black, his face filled with pain.

Adam was turned to face Harry.

"Python, teach him to choose manners," said Keenan.

Python? Not Harry? Adam was confused. They were using different names. What the hell was going on?

Harry, or Python, kneed Adam twice and then kicked him in the stomach. Adam coughed up something into the back of the handkerchief. His throat gurgled.

Near the brow of the hill, at the far end of a field, they stopped.

11:58 p.m.

Keenan pulled the leather-bound book and a long knife from his backpack.

Sofia smiled. "Go on."

"Yes, go on," said Harry. "Say the words of sacrifice."

The knife didn't glint. It was dark and solid.

The handkerchief was pulled from Adam's mouth. "I'll do anything," he burbled, panic making his brain spin like a wheel on ice. "Just don't kill me. I promise, anything."

11:59 p.m.

Keenan started. "Master, accept this sacrifice..."

Something flashed past the rim of Adam's vision and hit Sofia, who let out a small groan and fell to the ground. Suddenly the arm she had been holding was free.

What...?

Then a figure in a dark top threw himself into the group. The knife left Keenan's hands and twisted in the air before hitting the grass with a whisper.

Adam and Harry stood frozen for an instant, then Adam snapped himself loose and dived for the knife.

What happened next only took a second. Adam grabbed the knife, his mind blinded by panic and twisted by pain. In the same instant, Harry dived at him, drawing back his fist to punch. Adam could do nothing to stop him. Everything hung in slow motion for a moment, then sped up again.

The knife went into Harry. Immediately—too late—Adam's

hand leaped away from the hilt. He knew what had happened before Harry even fell to the ground.

He had killed him.

Beside him, the older boy in the black top had Keenan pinned to the ground, while Sofia sat on the grass, moaning in pain and clutching her head.

"Run," said the older boy to Adam. "Run! And if you ever need me again, I will be where you and the girl went through the water."

Adam immediately set off toward the festival site, oblivious to the impression he would make with red stains on his hands.

He didn't look back.

He had almost been killed.

He was a killer.

And he had left the knife—the knife with his fingerprints. Evidence of his guilt.

All around him, the trees and grass murmured accusingly as he ran on: *savage, killer, murderer.*

A loud and deep voice came back: "Will you shut up?" Then another voice: "Move on or I'm going to punch your lights out!"

"Meg!"

Then, in the distance, Megan's voice saying, "Adam? Ad—"

And the voice was cut off.

She was near, just a row or two away.

The music had now stopped, and here and there people were returning for the night. Adam ran down the rows, the rain heavier now, making the ground slippery. He noticed that the rain sliding from his hands onto the lamp had a red tinge. Proof of his crime.

Suddenly, in the distance, he saw the backs of Megan and Cassie. *Thank God.* A little flame of awareness flickered in his mind: *hide the case and prepare to fight.* He threw the case between two tents and put the lamp in his right hand. It was the best weapon he had.

The girls turned at that instant. "Adam, I'm *so* sorry," Megan said, clearly upset. "They said that they were going to send you to me as part of the game. I'm *really* sorry. I *knew* it was a bad idea."

"Yes, a bad idea," he said, looking at Cassie.

"Adam, *please* forgive me. I was really worried when I realized you'd gone." Megan was near to tears.

"It seems that things didn't work out," said Cassie.

Adam moved between the girls, pushing Megan slightly behind him, leaving a very faint red imprint on her top.

The rain fell heavily.

Walking toward Cassie, Adam growled, "Listen to me, you evil bitch." He gripped the lamp. Cassie cast a large shadow against a nearby tent.

"Adam, we really are sorry. It was stupid, *stupid*, and dumb," interrupted Megan. She was properly crying, her face contorted and her shoulders moving erratically up and down. "Please can we go back now?"

Cassie mimicked her: "Please can we go back now?"

Megan still cried, soaked and alone, as Adam moved closer to Cassie.

Adam spoke very deliberately, fear gone, anger composing him. "Cassie, or whatever your name is, I *promise* you that if you don't go, I will make you."

A million drops of rain drummed off tents and hard earth.

Cassie spoke equally slowly, but quietly, so not even Megan could hear: "If you have hurt Harry or anyone else, I will cause you so much pain that you will *beg* to die."

They stared at one another, bonded by hatred.

Megan came to Adam's side. "Please, *please* let's go back now. I want to go home."

Cassie moved away, unsmiling. "I'm sure we'll get to play truth or dare again sometime. . . ." Then she started to run.

Megan stood next to Adam in the dark as he washed his hands under the outside tap near to their tents. Her eyes were red with emotion and sudden fatigue. "What happened? Why are you washing your hands? I don't understand." She looked thin in her wet jumper and jeans. "And what's that?" she pointed at the case that Adam had retrieved.

Fear and guilt coiled like two snakes in Adam's mind. He started to shake.

"Megan, I would normally tell you anything. But I never want to talk about what happened tonight." He had never shouted at Megan before, *ever*, but he did now. There was real desperation in his voice. "Never, never. Have you got that?"

Megan's face splintered again into tears and confusion.

Adam stepped forward and put his arms around her. She stood still, like a pillar, arms at her side. Adam didn't say anything.

Megan didn't understand what Adam had done, but she knew that the hug meant he was sorry, and that he cared for her. But she still feared that something had happened to change their lives.

15

Adam didn't sleep at all that night. He was terrified of another attack, so he never actually put his head down. His tent was some way from Cassie's and Keenan's, and much nearer to the main road through the site, but sometimes a rustle rose above the drumming of the rain and Adam tightened his grip on the mallet used to drive in the tent pegs. He was in mortal danger. And he had done something terrible. He knew he should tell someone.

But how could he? He was a *killer.*

His parents were decent people, but they would immediately involve the police, which would lead to arrest and imprisonment, probably. Adam didn't really know what they did with thirteen-year-olds, but the words *Young Offenders' Institution* hung over him. Or maybe they would send him to a *home,* a Victorian building with brutal dormitories and metal beds and cold showers.

Adam saw his future dribbling away. He prodded the locked suitcase.

He certainly couldn't confide in anyone at school. He hardly knew his form teacher, Mrs. Hopkins. Mrs. Tavistock? No way. Mr. Sterling? He wouldn't be shocked to hear Adam had massacred a village, but even he would probably do what teachers do. It would all go straight back to parents and the police.

Asa or Leo? He kept all important things from them already. No, there was only one person: Megan. And he wanted to protect her from it all. He would have to do this on his own. If he kept quiet it would all go away—not immediately, but slowly; it would fade until it was just a shadow and might not have happened at all.

And in between thinking this, Adam kept being dragged back to fearful tension by the slightest noise.

Asa's shallow breathing continued regardless. Adam looked again at the case. Eventually he decided to take it behind the shower block and force it open with the mallet.

Megan didn't sleep at all that night, lying still in the darkness, turning the events of the evening over and over in her mind. Rachel asked several times what the matter was, but she always said the same thing: "I don't want to talk about it."

To complicate things further for Megan, Asa's dad had called her parents by walking to the gate and getting reception on his phone. The words *missing with Adam* would have conjured up all sorts of images in their minds. Asa's parents didn't ask many questions when Adam and Megan had finally arrived: they were tired and saw only a vague boyfriend–girlfriend situation. If only they had thought to investigate, things would have taken a very different course. But they didn't know how very ignorant they were, so didn't think to ask.

The rain and early start had kept most people awake, so Adam and Megan were among tired company the next morning. Adam felt wretched: worried, depressed, exhausted.

"Is everything okay?" asked Leo needlessly.

"I think that there's been a bit of a domestic," said Asa in front of Adam. "Let me know if you want some advice from

Uncle Asa." He was buoyed by his success with Rachel and had slept soundly.

As they packed up, Adam glanced across the field to where they had played Truth or Dare. How long ago that seemed. He couldn't make out individual tents very well, but almost all of them had been taken down. Still the metallic case sat at Adam's feet.

"Is that one yours?" asked Asa's dad, who seemed to have completely forgotten about the earlier events.

"Yes," he lied.

In silence, Adam and Megan walked to the station, trailing slightly behind the rest. As they left the festival site, the Rock Harvest banner still dripping from the overnight rain, Adam saw a tall blond boy and a brown-haired girl waiting in the distance by the roadside. Thinking about safety in numbers—they couldn't attack him *here*, surely—Adam drifted closer to the others, but gradually realized that they looked nothing like the pair he thought they were. His shoulders slumped and he suddenly felt desperate to get home.

Milton Keynes Station was awash with festival goers, a rather more subdued bunch than two or three days earlier. Somehow, everyone from Gospel Oak Senior had managed to gather in the middle of platform four, the departure point for one of the trains to London.

Adam and Megan wandered up. Jake was in the middle of the group. "I sorted him out," he was saying, "and he didn't bother us again." Adam felt safer now that he was with familiar faces, even Jake Taylor's.

Then something terrible. Across two tracks on the parallel platform was another familiar face: Cassie. She seemed to be alone and looked as tired as Adam.

Adam noticed a train about two hundred yards away, trundling closer with the usual sparks and squeaks, about to arrive in front of her.

She mouthed four words: "The case. Leave it."

Adam edged away from his group and spoke across the tracks, "Why?"

The train was gliding in. One hundred yards.

"I want it."

Adam waited, looking between case and girl.

Fifty yards.

He shrugged a little. "Okay."

Then twenty yards, then ten.

And at that point he threw the case toward Cassie, but it fell short, on to the tracks in front of her platform. Almost immediately the train was sitting over it like a dinosaur shielding an egg. There was no way that Cassie could get to it until the train pulled away.

Curious onlookers muttered and nudged, including some from Adam's group.

"Grant, you're so stupid," said Jake. "I've had dumps that are more intelligent than you. I don't know why a pretty thing like Meggie wastes her time with you." At that moment Adam's train arrived and they all flooded on.

Adam found himself able to look out of the window and see the train on Cassie's platform pull out, revealing the case.

Despite the shock of onlookers and shouts from attendants on the station, Cassie leaped onto the tracks. Adam peered down from his train.

With terrifying presence of mind, she glanced up and smiled. "Thanks." And, looking pretty, and innocent and attractive in ways that still affected Adam despite everything, she added, "See you soon."

Then, case in her arms, she leaped back up on to the platform. Several travelers gathered around her.

Seconds later she turned back toward Adam, fire in her eyes and snarling. She was looking for the fastest way to reach him.

Adam gave a weary smile from his train as it slowly pulled away.

She showed him the broken clasp on the case. Broken with a tent hammer.

Adam held up a large envelope in one hand and his backpack in the other.

Cassie, lips tight and fists clenched, shrieked and yelled at Adam's train window as it slid away down the track. The people near her backed away, confused and frightened.

Adam put the envelope in his bag. Inside was £1,000 in fifties and twenties. Cassie was not worried by the loss of the money. "Money is just paper," Coron would say, "and we can always get more." She was more worried by the loss of her weapon, now in Adam's backpack. But she was most worried by what Coron's reaction would be.

Not only did Adam live, but he now had a gun.

Megan looked on, realizing that something strange and dark had happened.

Adam was light-headed as he turned to Leo and sighed. *I'm a thirteen-year-old boy killer with a gun*, he thought. Not that he knew how to use it; Adam imagined waving it, looking threatening. They wouldn't know he was frightened by its cold, noisy, flesh-tearing potential. Once he was home safely he would drop it in the river, or hide it in the rubbish.

Home. I'll be safe soon, he thought. *They don't know who I am or where I live. It will all be over soon.*

Back on the platform, Cassie—Viper—watched the train amble away down the track to London. "You don't know who or what you're dealing with," she muttered.

16

"What! How?" Coron smashed his fist into his desk, then held his head in his hands. "The Master will make me suffer for this." He paused. "Someone has to pay—someone will have to be sacrificed."

Viper, Cobra and Asp stood in front of Coron. They were no longer three relaxed festival goers. "Cassie," "Keenan" and "Sofia" were now terrified servants. They knew what Coron could do. Fear and love of him were woven together in their minds.

"Where is Python's body?" Coron murmured.

Cobra, suddenly looking younger than his fifteen years, spoke first. "Marcia collected it when she picked us up. It's in the trunk of the car. We carried it from the Hill of Sacrifice to the lane on the far side."

"Sacrifice! Sacrifice? There will be sacrifice, believe me. Take the body downstairs," said Coron coldly. "Python failed me—and he failed the Master. Leave his body for us all to see. And he may yet be more use in death than he was in life." Coron looked at his hands, red from thumping the table. "How did this happen? Whose fault was it?"

"The Traitor appeared, Lord Coron." Cobra knew this news would not calm the situation: the Traitor was hated almost as much as the Imposter. "He came out of the darkness."

"What? I will have to deal with *him* myself!" Coron roared. "How could this happen? How?"

The room was silent again. Then a knock at the door. A figure half appeared.

Coron shouted: "I will kill anyone who interrupts me. Go!" Then he turned to the children. "I have been interrupted enough. Why have you failed me?"

The three looked at the floor.

"I want you to undo what you have done. Bring back Python, and kill…" Coron could hardly bring himself to say the name, "…kill *Adam*. The fact that he *again* escapes shows that he *is* the one."

Madness coursed through Coron. His mind had no limits. Insanity energized him, freed him from petty logic. He continued. "Go on! Reverse time, and make it different." The Master would make him suffer. Coron cultivated his madness so that he could hide inside it.

Asp, who was fifteen, but looked more than a year younger than the other two, decided to speak. "There was nothing we could do."

"Nothing? *Nothing?* Nothing will come of nothing." Coron laughed hysterically for about fifteen seconds. "Nothing? I want to know who was responsible."

"I can tell you, my lord Coron," Viper said. "It was *Asp.* She should have stayed with the girl, and I should have gone with Adam. It only went wrong when she got involved."

Asp frowned and turned. "But you said—"

"I think that she is not truly… not truly one of *us*," said Viper.

"My lord, I would do anything…" started Asp.

Coron raised his palm slowly and calmly. "Viper, what you say is a strange and dreadful thing. But I have long thought we had another traitor in the camp. A dog waiting to bite us. Someone who is not what they seem." Ideas were quickly forming in his mind; unconnected links were fusing. Coron whispered, "It is the *only* way to explain the failure. There must be another traitor."

Yes, he thought. *Another virus to be eliminated.*

Asp whimpered, "It isn't true. Look at my head. Look—I was hit."

Cobra spoke now, clearly, authoritatively. "I too had my doubts about Asp. I feared the truth. I think she *enjoyed* the world out there."

Coron put his hands together and pressed them to his chin. "Asp. Asp. If you confess, you will be shown mercy."

Asp felt that she was in a cave—a damp, bare and isolated hole. She thought of her time at the festival. They had all enjoyed it, hadn't they? But she had done wrong. Coron would save her. He would show mercy. She looked at Coron. "Yes, I did take some enjoyment from the world."

"I knew it," said Coron. "How much?"

"Some." She thought again. "More than a bit."

"I see. And you worked with the Traitor?"

"No," she said. "That isn't true. I didn't do that."

"Asp, my dear, dear child—" he smiled slightly—"it will help if you confess. It will make things less...ugly."

Asp thought hard. She was unsure what to say. The lie would help, surely. Coron was always right, but she had to help herself. Just this once.

She took a risk. "Yes," she said, nervously and hopefully. "I sort of worked with him."

Coron relaxed. "And you loved him?"

This is working, Asp thought. "No. Not that. Not like I love you."

"And you went to him?"

"No!"

Coron stood up and approached Asp. He stroked her hair, then held her face with both hands. He now saw only treachery. To Coron, her denials were proof of how twisted she was. "Beautiful and wicked Asp. Clever Asp. How you have disappointed us." He squeezed tighter; Asp found it hard to breathe. "Why? Why? Why? Why?" he repeated. She was desperate for breath now, but dared not reach out to Coron; to push him away would be a terrible thing.

Still gripping tight—*I need to breathe,* thought Asp—Coron told Cobra and Viper to take hold of her. Then he let go. Asp gulped in wonderful air.

"I want you to help me take Asp up to Dorm Thirteen," Coron said. "Where she will stay. Permanently."

"But..."—*NO!*—"You said there would be mercy," she whispered.

Coron put his finger to her lips. "Shhh." He paused. "*God* will show mercy when you meet him." The hint of a laugh. "And I may offer you mercy too."

Asp was dragged through corridors and up flights of stairs by the older two. She cried and begged; she struggled and shook.

Surely this is not going to happen, she thought.

All too soon they arrived at a white door. The number thirteen was painted on it in coarse, blotchy black paint.

She had never seen inside.

Coron opened the door.

It is going to happen, she realized.

The square room had no windows and was empty apart from a light sunk into the ceiling. Three small circular grilles were visible on each of the walls.

She knew what happened in Dorm Thirteen. She had heard from others.

Asp was thrown in. *Even now,* she thought, *Coron might change his mind.*

"A little mercy," Coron said, and Asp's heart leaped. Coron pulled something from behind him, from his belt. "Here—for you."

He threw a small gun to the far end of the room, beyond Asp.

"There is one bullet in the chamber. You may use it. Or you can stay here *permanently*."

He shut the door. *Click.* It was locked.

As Coron, Viper and Cobra walked back down the stairs, they heard beating on the thick door and a faint, dreadful, desperate wail.

"Good," said Coron. "Now we can turn our attention to Adam."

Viper and Cobra nodded and smiled.

17

Adam knelt by the side of his bed, curtains closed, door locked. Set out in front of him was a gun and £1,000 in notes—the contents of the case taken from the festival.

The death was imprinted on his every thought, like a watermark running through everything in the world. *How did I get in this position? (I killed someone.) Why didn't I drop the knife? (I killed someone.) How will I tell the police? (I killed someone.) How will I tell my parents?*

He poked the gun with his finger as if it was an animal that would bite. Then he picked it up. It was smaller than he imagined, not much more than seven inches by five, and lighter—it weighed about as much as a big block of cheese. It was also colder than he'd expected. Icy cold.

Now that he had it, he was reluctant to let it go. What if they knew where he lived? He might have to defend himself and his parents. But he had no idea how to use a gun. Did he just pull the trigger? He had heard the expression *safety catch* in films. Would it be loud? He didn't even know if it was loaded.

Adam saw the word *Walther* at the bottom of the handle, just below his little finger. It sounded vaguely familiar, probably from a film. Folding his duvet over gun and money, he pulled his laptop across from his desk.

He typed in some keywords. After a few minutes he understood.

"Oh my God," whispered Adam. It held lots of bullets. In films and songs guns often had glamour, but Adam felt depressed and desperate. His natural inclination was still to tell his parents and go to the police. He had killed in self-defense, surely. Self-defense isn't murder, is it? He hadn't really decided to kill. Or had he?

His mum's voice came through the door. "Adam, I can see your light on. After the weekend you've had you need to get some sleep. I think I'll take your computer away." She tried the locked door. "Adam, are you on Facebook again?"

Adam silently took the gun and money and put them under his bed, then went to the door, computer in hand. "Sorry, Mum."

"Adam, is everything okay? You don't look your usual self."

This was the moment. He could tell her now.

Adam let the moment slide away until it was out of reach. "I'm fine," he said, his tone trying to give the smallest hint that he was not.

Before he climbed into bed, Adam hid the gun again, submerging it in a big tub of Legos that he hadn't opened in years. Then he pulled back the curtains for a glance at Megan's house.

He couldn't see clearly in the darkness, but Megan was looking at his house too. She knew that something strange had happened, and tomorrow would insist on understanding what it was. She grabbed her phone and quickly sent a text: "c u tomoz. Luv m."

Less than a minute later her phone pinged: "Soz for way things are. C u. Love ad."

She smiled. He had written *love* in full. How great.

The next morning, Adam was in the shed near the bushes at the bottom of his garden when Megan passed by. She saw a ghost-like figure through the dusty window: Adam.

"Here we go," Adam muttered.

"What are you doing in *here*?" she asked, the door squeaking as she opened it.

"Um, looking for some nails."

"Why?" Megan knew it was a lie. Nails? How ridiculous.

"Er, to mend the fence," he said unconvincingly. If only he could lie better than this.

"Mend the fence?" she said, hands on hips. "Adam, what's going on?"

"Nothing."

"Adam, what happened at the festival? I can't think of anything else; I want to know. Why was there red on your hands?" Megan avoided saying *blood*. "I know you were in a fight."

"Nothing. Don't know."

In frustration and with a sudden spike of anger, Megan raised her voice: "I've been grounded for not getting back on time at the festival, but I still came over here to look for you and now all you can do is lie. We've never had secrets before. What's changed?"

"I'm not lying." Adam shrugged. He hated being like this, but wanted to protect her.

Then Megan stepped forward and slapped him, hard. His ear, neck and cheek stung. "You liar!" she shouted. "You bloody liar! Why won't you tell me?" She looked as if she was about to strike again.

"Meg. I can't. And don't shout," Adam said, gesturing for her to keep quiet.

"Adam," she said, more quietly, "who is your best friend?"

"Oh, Meg. Please don't do this to me. You know that it's you."

"Then tell me what's going on."

Adam was torn by indecision. He didn't want to tell Megan, but he had to tell someone. The secret burned within him like a fiery coal.

Adam reached up and pulled down a slightly rusty Quality Street tin from the shelf. He showed Megan what he had hidden inside: £1,000. She was wide-eyed, then frowned. He whispered to her about the gun and the suitcase.

Megan went pale; her hands shook.

But a worse truth had to be told. Adam beckoned her to sit down on the dusty floor, below window height. Then he began whispering, coldly detached from the story, telling it as if it was a film he had seen, as if he was talking about someone else. He told it in order. At the very end he had to say the awful words: "He fell on the knife. He was trying to kill me. But I killed him."

Megan stared.

"Meg, did you hear me? I've killed someone."

They looked at one another.

"There's no doubt. There was blood, and he fell down. And the knife went right in. Meg—I didn't push it, honestly I didn't. I would do anything to take that moment back."

Megan had not interrupted once. Now she said just two words: "Oh no."

"Meg, I'm a murderer. My whole life is ruined."

Adam then watched her cry for about half a minute. He desperately wanted to hug her. Surprisingly, she didn't criticize or ask questions; she didn't respond at all as an adult would. And as soon as her tears stopped, she was practical, sensible, serious: "You *have* to tell your parents and go to the police. It was self-defense. They were going to *kill* you. These people might come back. What are you going to do then? Shoot them all?"

He looked deep into her blue eyes. "Okay. I'll tell my parents this evening." And with his hand on her shoulder, the words came out very formally: "Meg...thank you."

Megan twisted around so that she faced Adam, then touched the side of his head, above his stinging ear, now more like a caring adult than a girl, and gently pressed for several seconds. "Adam..." She paused again. "I'll always be your friend."

* * *

That evening, at about 9:45 p.m., Adam took the gun from the Lego tub, intending to explain everything to his parents. He knew that walking in with a gun in his hand would be an awful and life-changing moment, but then found he was so terrified about what would happen next that he couldn't make an entrance at all.

A bit longer, just a bit longer, he thought.

A black Range Rover with four people in it swept along deserted country lanes. The people inside were silent, full of dreadful purpose. Scarred palms held the steering wheel; a woman in the passenger seat picked at her short nails; two teenagers sat in the back, flint-faced. Bony trees were lit for a time by headlights, then passed in a blur.

Adam sat in his room. 10:45 p.m. became 11:45 p.m.

Wheels spun quickly down a two-lane road, then even faster down a highway. London: fifteen miles. Exit at the next junction, said the sign.

Adam decided that at midnight he would knock on his parents' bedroom door. That would give him fifteen more minutes of freedom.

Smaller roads, lined by houses and trees. The Range Rover stopped. The four people stepped out, all of them carrying backpacks.

Midnight came and went, and Adam still hadn't spoken to his parents. Now it was 1:00 a.m., and he realized it would have to wait until tomorrow. It was too late. A few hours wouldn't make any difference.

*   *   *

The four walked across a park. A voice came from the gloom. "Hey," someone was calling. "Hey!" Three men emerged from what looked like a children's playground. "Are you lost?" There was laughter. "Out for a walk?"

Coron responded, speaking into the darkness from under one of the lights that were strung along the path. "I think you should leave us alone."

More laughter from the three potential muggers. "No, I think *you* should leave *us* alone." The men jogged to the path, indistinct shadows vaguely lit by no more than a half-moon and the glow of the city. Arriving into the limited circle of light, one of the men spoke aggressively: "Hand everything over and no one will get hurt."

Coron looked dismissive. He took a deep breath. "You have picked the wrong people."

"We're so, so scared," mocked the tallest of the three. "You've just met the wrong people. Don't try to be brave, Daddy." He pulled a knife. "You're pissing me off."

Coron was calm. "Do you have bad dreams?"

"What?"

"Welcome to a nightmare."

Coron grabbed one of the muggers; Marcia another. They were bundled to the floor, almost invisible in the darkness. There was scuffling, followed by five or six dull thuds. Then silence.

The remaining mugger, suddenly confused and wary, stared at Viper and Cobra. He saw that these teenagers were also calm. Why?

Viper spoke. "Thieves shouldn't play with murderers."

Murderers? What was this?

Coron and Marcia returned, surrounding the thief. Gripping the mugger's head, Coron whispered in his ear, "Remember my name: Coron. Mention it."

"What? Who to? Who should I tell?" he stammered.

"Our New God. You're about to meet him."

At 2:00 a.m. Adam lay down on his bed. I'll speak to Mum and Dad first thing in the morning, he thought. I know that they love me; it'll be all right. He fell into an exhausted sleep. He would be awake within the hour.

In the park, three young men were found dead the next morning. One, propped against a tree, had not died quickly.

18

At 2:40 a.m. Coron, Marcia, Viper and Cobra reached Adam's house.

They had spent the previous morning in the gym preparing and rehearsing. Coron was both director and leader. He had over one hundred willing servants, but the Master had told *him* to be his avenging angel, just like the angel who had killed the firstborn in Egypt. The Master's Angel. *God's Angel.*

Archangel Coron. Yes, that was his destiny.

Coron said that the Traitor would be somewhere nearby, so they hoped for a second kill. "It will be one of the greatest nights in history if both are eliminated," Coron had said to the assembly at the Old School House. But there was no one around to witness them striding down the path to Adam's garden.

They slipped through the bushes and toward the house in single file, a mere rustle of movement that was lost among other sounds that litter a night. Then backpacks were opened with clasps, rather than zippers, for silence. Four identical containers were pulled out and unscrewed. The smell of gasoline rose.

The sweet smell of gasoline, thought Coron. The sweet smell of death. Leading to the sweeter smell of a burnt offering. An odor that would rise up to the Master—and to God.

Viper and Cobra thought of past kills. Like hunters, they were greedy for another. But with Adam they wanted more.

They wanted revenge; for him to be frightened and say *please, stop*; for him to hurt.

Coron put his duplicate key into the back door. It wouldn't go in fully. The original key was in the lock on the inside.

Cobra stepped forward, pulling a small screwdriver from his backpack. If this didn't work, he would break a window. But that was a coarse and noisy method. They were not common criminals.

Ninety seconds later they were in.

The four slipped through to the sitting room. Silence— apart from the usual *tocks* and *buzzes* that are common to every house. For two or three seconds the fridge rattled, then was still. Adam's fish drifted around their tank, dumb witnesses to the four intruders.

Coron spoke quietly, below a whisper: "Of all the people in the world, we are the *most* important. Nothing will happen tonight that is more significant than what *we* will do here." He closed his eyes. "Master, we serve you."

An equally quiet response came back, not much more than the movement of lips: "We serve you, Coron; we serve the Master; and we serve the New God."

The four went in separate directions. Viper and Marcia splashed gasoline downstairs, while Coron and Cobra did upstairs.

Glug. Glug. Gasoline was spilled, carefully, thoughtfully, arteries linking to veins. *We are like artists*, thought Viper as she poured spill after spill over the sofas. They pulled threads to weave in the most flammable material. Skilled work in the service of the Master.

Coron and Cobra did the same on the stairs and landing. Quiet spurts of gas, soaking into carpet, seeping under doors, spreading like thin molasses.

Finally, Coron reached Adam's door.

Coron had intended to stop there. But something stirred in his spirit. A desire to torment his victim.

With his head pressing against the sign that said Adam's Room, Coron pushed down the handle and opened the door.

Even imposters must sleep, Coron thought. Even Adam must sleep.

The smell of gasoline was strong now, and Adam was beginning to stir. Coron went forward three paces and quickly put his hand over Adam's mouth and nose.

Adam was drifting out of sleep, swimming up into the place where dreams blend with reality, where consciousness is seen above like ripples on the surface of a pool.

Panic filled Adam the instant he realized he couldn't breathe. He couldn't think of anything else, just the need for oxygen. Then some air crept in, and with it a spasm of realization: there was a man here. Adam's eyes sprang open. The guy from the festival—Keenan—was behind the man.

Adam tried to scream, but a hand was clasped over his mouth. Nothing came out but a long and throaty "mmm" sound; spent air filled his lungs.

The hand relaxed. Air. Gas, thought Adam.

"Hello, Adam. I am the avenging angel, come to kill the firstborn of the millennium."

"Let me go," Adam choked out. Predictable, natural, futile words.

"No. I don't think so. You are the thirteenth, and you are thirteen; if you become fourteen, you become a man, and if you become a man, then the world will not have the leader it needs. Me."

There was no strange look or mad tone. This man was not the Joker or the Green Goblin. There was nothing comic book about him. His words were blunt and simple, as if he thought they were obvious.

Surely someone who spoke so calmly would have some sense of reason. So Adam said, "Please, I think you need help. If we could just think about this..."

Another hand, slightly smaller and less abrasive, pushed hard into Adam's face, forcing his lips against his teeth. Then Adam felt breathing on his ear. It was Cobra. "We are going to start the burning now, and it will continue for eternity."

Coron whispered again, standing up. "You see, fire is like an idea. It spreads slowly at first, but gathers pace and enthusiasm. Eventually it makes the world roar. *I* will make the world roar. I am the chosen one."

He pulled a packet of matches from his pocket. Adam could barely make out the box in the dark, but he heard the familiar rattle of the thin sticks inside.

Cobra pushed his left hand hard into Adam's throat, shoving and squeezing with the strength that hatred gives. His right hand held plastic cord-like handcuffs. "You will see death coming." Adam felt his throat close.

"Bind him," said Coron. "We offer you as a burnt sacrifice to the Master." Coron pulled out a match and rested its head against the side of the box.

Cobra smiled and giggled.

Then Coron lit the match and held it up in his left hand. A small flame flickered, a flame that would feast on gasoline.

Suddenly a familiar voice, full of horror and confusion, came from the doorway: Adam's dad. He shouted, "Oh my God—help—get out—Adam!"

Adam saw Coron pull a gun from his inside pocket with his right hand.

For an instant, all was still. The match burned unwavering in Coron's left hand as he murmured, "Shhhh."

Before Adam realized what was happening, there was a snapping sound from the gun, followed by a thud as Adam's dad staggered backward and fell to the ground. His dad made short gasping sounds: "Ad-am; Ad-am."

Adam twisted and writhed against Cobra's grasp, desperate to get to his father.

The match was now half-burned, still upright, without a tremble, between Coron's fingers. Only a lunatic would have such conviction when faced with another's death.

Dark specks were appearing in front of Adam's eyes. He was losing consciousness. Some specks became blotches. Cobra was dragging him out of bed and down to the floor to tie him up.

Coron stepped into the hallway, put his foot on Adam's dad and spat, "You protected Adam. You are also an enemy of the Master." But the match had burned down into Coron's fingers and gone out. Adam heard the scrape and fizz of a new flame.

There was a bump as Adam hit the floor. Cobra readied his cuffs and glanced down to Adam's hands. He stared: Adam was holding a gun—the gun from the metal case.

It was harder for Adam to pull the trigger than he had anticipated, but almost immediately there was a loud cracking sound and Cobra breathed in and went rigid.

Adam squeezed again and Cobra slumped on top of him.

A lit match spiralled from Coron's hand, over and over, perhaps eight times, the flame alternately growing and shrinking, until it hit the floor and a pool of fire illuminated him.

Just like the devil, Adam thought as he raised the gun. *Fiery and hellish.* Lying on the floor, even with Cobra on his left side, he was able to look down the line of fire. He vaguely aimed for Coron's torso and forced his finger to squeeze again. This time the gun was hard to keep still; it leaped back and up.

The bullet cut through the air—*whoosh*—and impacted into Coron's right arm, halfway between elbow and shoulder.

Coron dropped his gun into the gathering flames.

All the time dancing yellow was spreading along the lines of gas.

Adam saw his mum in the smoke-filled hallway behind Coron, who turned. For an instant there was hesitation, then Coron rushed forward, hoisted his uninjured arm and punched her with a single blow, knocking her to the ground.

Viper appeared at the top of the stairs. "There's someone forcing the front door. Should we kill them?"

Coron turned back toward Adam's room, where smoke was now turning from mist to fog. Behind him flames hopped down the stairs step by step. He thought of the gun in Adam's hand. Even in Coron's mind, a thin line of logic tugged him toward self-preservation. "No. We must go."

When the flames reached the bottom of the stairs they spread out in six different directions, and the room was quickly ablaze.

Adam went to his father and beat at the sparks on his pajama trousers. His mother was smothered by smoke; flames crept closer to her. He tugged—"Dad, please move!"—eliciting a small groan.

Three figures left by the back door, one clutching his arm, and dashed through the garden; they coughed as they sprinted along the small path, each step taking them farther from the glimmering yellow of Adam's house.

Inside, smoke was filling Adam's lungs. He pushed open the bathroom door: no fire—the tentacles of gas not having reached there—but smoke flooded in as Adam dragged his father next to the bath.

The house began to crackle.

Adam closed the bathroom door and ran to his mother. She coughed quietly. "Adam?"

Adam began to drag her down the stairs through flame and smoke. It was useless. The carpet was on fire. She was too heavy and he felt faint. He leaned against the wall on the stairs, nudging a photo. He wanted to close his eyes and go to sleep.

Then he heard someone shouting, "Come on!"

It was the teenager who had saved him before. Was Adam dreaming? Why was he here again?

Again the same voice, shrieking with urgency: "Come on!"

Flames lapped like waves as together they dragged Adam's mother out. Heat embraced them. Piercing heat. Burning heat.

They fell out of the back door, heaving for breath. Three or four neighbors had appeared, and there were shouts and calls for help. "Fire—we need help!" a man yelled into his cell phone.

Awoken by the noise, Megan looked out the window. Seeing an orange glow and smoke painting itself against the darker night sky, she ran.

Adam looked at the neighbors. "My dad! He's still in there." He started to go back.

Someone held him. "You can't go in there. You'll kill yourself."

Staring at the house, Adam fought to get closer. "My dad!" He broke free and ran toward the door.

The boy who had helped him pull out his mother blocked his way. "You'll die, Adam!"

"I'm getting my dad!" Adam kicked and screamed, but the older boy was strong. Precious seconds passed. Smoke billowed from windows and heat-reddened faces.

"Let me go!" Adam shouted. "Let me in!"

"You stay," the boy said as he shoved Adam back, then ran into the black cloud that poured through the door.

Confusion, noise, smoke, fire.

Megan tore across the garden. "Adam! Adam!"

Adam looked at the burning house, desperation smothering him, and roared and roared, an echo of the fire.

Suddenly, the bathroom window was open, and through the smoke Adam saw one person holding another—dragging, desperately heaving toward the window.

People looked around for something to break their fall. Nothing. There was nothing.

Can't someone do something? Smoke and flames were hungry for victims. Large snaps, like branches being torn in two. Thousands of hisses turned to small explosions.

Adam's father fell like a stone and, despite the efforts of a neighbor to catch him, crashed through a plastic garden table below. The boy let himself down as far as he could, then leaped, his fall becoming a roll as he hit the ground.

Sparks fizzed and spun through the air.

Adam's dad was dragged across the grass like a heavy sack. Adam fought through the throng of neighbors and leaned close. His dad was making a noise at the back of his throat—a long thin wailing sound.

Two medics ran from an ambulance and appeared around the side of the house.

Much farther away, three shadowy figures ran toward a Range Rover.

19

As paramedics rushed to Adam's parents, neighbors tried to assist and reassure him—"Stand back.... Give them some air.... Don't worry...."—but the only comfort to Adam was Megan's silent presence.

The fire was a frenzied parasite, embracing and consuming all before it. Smoke poured from windows and seeped through tiles. Near the gutters, flames reached out like fingers trying to prise open the roof. Then there was a larger crash above the background of sizzling crackles as the fire leaped onto the top of the house, dancing in victory.

Firemen arrived, calling into radios: "The building is well alight. Make pumps five."

Adam knelt next to his mother. Her blonde hair was singed black, her burned skin drawn tight beneath an oxygen mask. She looked at Adam, her eyes widening slightly, the closest she could come to a reassuring smile. Adam simply put his hand on hers. She would understand.

Adam went to his father. The paramedic beside him was confused by the range of injuries, one of which was clearly a gunshot. The boy who'd rescued Adam was saying something that sounded very grown-up: "...isn't life-threatening if pressure is applied...bullet passed through..."

Adam knelt again. "Come on, Dad. You'll be fine," he said, but he wanted to hug his father instead of speaking to him. Megan put her arm around Adam's shoulder as he stood up.

Adam looked at the boy who had entered the building, the boy who had helped his parents, the boy who had saved him *twice*. "Thank you. I don't know who you are, but thank you so much."

More paramedics arrived. Two of them ran straight to Adam's father. "We need to get him to the hospital immediately. Get a stretcher. *Now*."

At the same time, three police officers jogged in: two women from the front of the house and a man who came up the garden from the bushes and the path. "You must clear this garden now," ordered one of the women. "Move out and stand back. This building is not safe."

The house blazed, casting a hot yellow glow over everyone.

Adam vaguely recognized the policeman. He had seen him at the station.

"Your parents will be fine," the officer said in the way that adults do to children. "It's Adam, isn't it? My name is Chief Inspector Hatfield." He turned to the young man. There was surprise, perhaps even shock, and immediate recognition.

Adam knew that he was no longer the sole focus of attention.

"Let's move him out," a paramedic was saying in the background.

"And what is your name?" said the chief inspector, his voice even, but with a hint of mockery.

The boy gave a low, monotone reply—something indistinct.

"I'm very keen to know where you live now."

"These days I have no fixed address."

"Well, I think you should come with me." The chief inspector reached for a pair of handcuffs that were dangling from his belt.

Adam interrupted, putting his arm out to stop the policeman. "No. There's some mistake. This guy saved us all. He went into the building. He's a hero."

Sparks blew across the garden.

"You know I'll not come willingly," warned the boy.

"It's me that you want," Adam said insistently, no longer caring, wanting it all to end. *I am the one who has killed again.*

The older boy turned toward him; "No, Adam, that's not right. You're still in—"

Chief Inspector Hatfield pounced on Adam's rescuer, calling for help. "This young man is under arrest." The pair twisted and shoved as he struggled to get the handcuffs in place. "Help! He is resisting arrest!"

Adam was confused. Normally, respect for the police would have beaten all other logic, but this person had saved his parents. "Let him go!" he shouted and grabbed the handcuffs, yanking them away.

Megan pleaded, "Adam! Stay out of it, *please.*"

The sight of a fight against the backdrop of the burning house transfixed onlookers. The two were silhouetted like shadow puppets, trading punches.

Adam shoved the policeman, enabling the older boy to deliver a flurry of kicks and punches. Then, darting between firemen and over hoses, pushing past paramedics and barging one of the other police officers, the boy disappeared, sprinting down the side of the house toward the road.

Adam stood outside the door of his father's hospital room. He gazed at the words *Intensive Care. Intensive.* Words echoed in his ears: "He will live, but there's a long journey ahead." Then a woman's voice: "Your mother is fine, but she will be here for some time." The sentences overlapped and became jumbled up in Adam's head. He didn't know what the doctors really thought; he reckoned they always managed to generate positive news when talking to kids. They skimmed off and delivered the encouraging bits and left the rest to brood menacingly.

Adam was standing with Megan and her parents. Megan's dad, Mr. James, was pulling his hand down his cheek, making a rasping sound over thin stubble. "I've spoken to the police, who've spoken to social services, and they say that you should come back with us, Adam. They'll want to talk to you tomorrow. There was an intruder who set fire to your house, and it seems that they shot your father."

I don't care that you're stating the obvious, thought Adam. *I'm going to need help.*

Mrs. James looked at her watch. "Let's try to get a couple of hours of sleep."

"I think there's something you should know," said Adam, looking at the floor, then glancing up.

"Yes?"

Adam stopped. There was something about the way Megan was looking at him. "Oh, nothing. I'm just tired. It's been horrible." His voice trailed off. It was better to explain everything to the police tomorrow.

Sitting in the back of the car with Megan as they drove back, Adam had a chance to worry about what was going to happen next. He had seen a program about forensic science and knew that the police would soon discover bones and guns. They would be poking around and taking away samples in small plastic bags. The guns would not have been burned away, that was certain. They also had ways to work out how fires started. Perhaps they would think that *he* was responsible. Adam seemed to remember a story about a girl who had killed her parents by burning their house down.

Why has everything gone wrong?

He gazed out of the window: shuttered shops and empty pavements drifted past. Then he felt a hand next to his. The little finger touched his thumb, just for a second.

It slipped away as Mrs. James turned around. "Adam, dear," she said. Megan's mum was not usually the sort of person to say *dear.* "You go in the spare room, the one opposite Meggie's. I'll find some clothes for you."

Clothes. Things. Adam had only thought about his parents.

Of course, he had lost everything in the fire. *Everything.* Or almost everything—an image of a Quality Street tin containing £1,000 quickly formed in his mind, then dissolved.

For a fearful thought took its place: he was still in danger, and those he was with were in danger. Below that there was an ocean of worry. Adam had killed twice now.

They entered Megan's house in silence. The smell of burning wafted across the gardens, reminding and threatening, though no one mentioned it.

Adam saw Megan once, when she left the bathroom and opened his door, saying his name. He was getting ready for bed. He liked it that Megan never knocked and waited.

"The bathroom's free. See you tomorrow."

"Thanks. I'm really grateful, Meg, but this is going to be complicated."

"Well, I'm here to help."

Then she spoke much louder as she went to her room: "'Night Mum, 'night Dad."

Adam closed his eyes. He wanted to think of something positive and calming. He tried to think of his parents, safe in the hospital. Then he tried to think of Megan: the way that she giggled and leaned toward him; the way that she had touched his hand.

But his mind was always dragged back to one image: a gun resting on a pile of bones, the charred remains of a teenager. Another gun nearby. Both in his bedroom. Would they think that he had shot his own father? The James's spare room faced away from his house, but he could still hear the rumbling of machinery and the shouting of firemen dousing the smouldering timbers. He imagined a jet of water spraying on cinders and revealing a gun underneath. *A gun resting on bones.*

Adam slept for nearly three hours, then woke with a start.

Two streets away, a boy with a scar crept past cars. Crouching down, he edged toward blue flashing lights and the throbbing of engines and pumping water.

A long vehicle with a ladder on its back was reversing past him, its *beep-beep* shouting *look out*. The word *Simon*, his own name and the make of the machine, was written on the side of the ladder in large black letters.

He could see two police officers ahead on the opposite side of the road, outside what remained of Adam's house. One of them was Chief Inspector Hatfield, who would be looking for him. And here he was, hidden behind a vehicle made by a company called Simon.

Chief Inspector Hatfield certainly knew that was his name.

Simon vaulted a gate and waited; through a small gap in the hedge he could see a fire engine. Hatfield was still in the distance. Simon saw that the fire was out, but steam and wisps of smoke still rose from the skeleton of the building.

The ability to wait had always served him well. He had been taught to take no unnecessary risks. *If waiting reduces risk— wait.* So he was patient.

A fireman, distinguished by his white rather than yellow helmet, came to Hatfield and said something. There was pointing and gesturing, and they went into what used to be Adam's front garden, stepping over the thick snakes that still carried water into the house.

Simon took his opportunity and scampered forward, running along the pavement and then down the side of the building opposite Adam's. He came to a neglected yard that housed bins, rusting fridges and moldy sofa cushions, then pushed open the back door and ran up three flights of stairs, taking them two at a time. At the top on the left was flat six. Simon had been lucky to find a room so close to Adam's house.

Blue flashed through thin curtains, giving just enough light to see. Simon didn't want to turn on the bare bulb.

The room was almost empty. A single mattress, with a pillow but no sheets, lay on the floor, and there was an old table and two chairs.

Everything was as Simon had left it when he'd seen the

smoke and dashed across to Adam's house. Now he quickly added a computer to the clothes already in his backpack, and picked up his mobile phone. In the bathroom he collected essentials. Then he felt the side of the backpack for other items. Satisfied, he pulled out his phone and typed a text, just thirteen words long.

SEND.

The message traveled from phone to mast to message center to mast to phone in an instant. It arrived at a number Simon had discovered after sliding Asa's phone from his pocket one morning on the tube.

The phone Simon wanted to send the message to had melted a few hours earlier. So he had to contact another one. But this receiving phone sat lifeless.

It was turned off, as her mum and dad insisted, in Megan's bedside cabinet, eighteen inches from her sleeping head.

No bleep; no red flashing light. The message was not received for nearly twelve hours.

20

Viper leaned across the back seat, pressing a cloth to Coron's right arm, as Marcia swung the car into the drive at the Old School House.

Coron held a phone in his left hand: "I want it brought in today." Something was being explained on the other end of the line. "No," Coron continued, "all of it. I am aware of the dangers. I want to be able to take us wherever the Master leads. Are you doubting us?"

The gates automatically closed behind them. As always, guards and weapons were nearby. On this occasion, anyone looking into the trees on the right-hand side would have seen a guard lurking behind a tree with a Heckler & Koch MP7 submachine gun.

The car slid to a stop. "I'll get Dr. Graves," said Marcia.

Something stirred within Coron. Marcia was attractive, and she cared. Coron shoved the feeling away. "That is exactly why we have failed," he shouted. "Why I have failed. Priorities."

Blood had stained through the cloth that Coron threw to the ground. The wound gave a severe, deep throb; lines of agony splintered through his arm. Coron felt as if several knives were pressing deep into him at once. But he relished the pain. It was as if his mind was being tugged toward it. *A punishment.* Coron pushed down slightly on to the gash: electric stinging pulsed outward. He squeezed more, digging in, and an explosion of blistering pain drove through bone and flesh.

Good. I want it to hurt.

Dr. Graves, summoned from her shift at the local hospital, gave instructions as Coron was laid on the table. She examined his shoulder, front and back, pressing around the wound and then opening it up slightly with her fingers. "I will have to extract the bullet," she said. "It's lodged deep."

Coron seemed unconcerned by the injury, though blood now covered his entire left side down to his knee and was smeared thinly over half his face.

Dr. Graves prepared medical instruments. "This is going to hurt. I'll give you something for the pain, but you may feel light-headed." Pressing the wound with one hand, she picked up a syringe with the other.

Coron turned his head so that he looked into the doctor's eyes. "No. No drugs. Never."

"Yes, Lord Coron." Dr. Graves eased the flesh apart; blood spread across the table and trickled onto the floor in steady drips. She used tweezers to extract the bullet, pushing deep into the raw gash. Coron closed his eyes and said nothing. He didn't flinch, even when the bullet was pulled from sinew and the pain throbbed and jabbed from deep within his shoulder.

The room was in silence.

When he heard the bullet clink on the table next to him, Coron emerged from his trance, half ignoring, half embracing the pain that screamed at him.

Viper admired Lord Coron's mastery of pain's intense bite. His bravery made her love him more than ever.

Coron walked through the main door and into a small room that was little more than a cupboard. His bandaged arm hung by his side. With his good arm, he pulled back a musty curtain and then opened a second door. This next room was much larger and had a polished wooden floor. Angled ceiling lights illuminated paintings that hung in every space, even in front of boarded-up windows.

He strode across the room, heading for a smaller door, pointed at the top, probably from an old church.

Coron did not look at the paintings, but those dragged screaming and pleading through this room did. The more unwilling and frightened they were, the more they noticed and understood. They saw Abraham lifting a knife above Isaac, a copy of a painting by Rembrandt; they saw Jephthah sacrificing his daughter in flames; they saw a large depiction of Josiah offering human bones on an altar.

Near the door that Coron opened there were more confusing and recent pictures: a figure falling in front of a tube train, a boy in his bed. And there were many others.

Every single picture portrayed sacrifice.

Coron closed the door behind him, revealing space for one final picture on the wall.

Words ran around the top of the room: "I will deliver you into the hands of brutal men who are skillful to destroy. You shall be the fuel for the fire; your blood shall be in the midst of the land."

Coron walked down a spiral staircase, through a door at the end of a small chamber and into a large space lit by thirteen candles. A black cloak was waiting for him.

He knelt down in front of a stone altar and closed his eyes. "Master, I am sorry."

The darkness in front of Coron seemed to dissolve. His mind scratched at the surface of reality, uncovering what lay beneath. Soon, like a face appearing on the surface of a swamp, Coron saw the Master emerging. He took shape in Coron's mind, growing, solidifying, edges being cut out of the air.

In the Middle Ages those who had visions were considered inspired.

As before, the same hallucination appeared, a wrinkled face

deeply lined like an old man's; then hair, in long tufts; then a thin, bony body almost covered by a cloak.

The Master was present.

They said that drugs would stop me seeing the Master. They were evil men who deserved their death.

"Master, I have failed you, and I will take whatever consequence you choose."

"Yes, you have failed. Adam is the one. He *must* be killed while he is still thirteen."

Coron knew this with a conviction even stronger than before. He had *always* known. *Adam* was the one. *Thirteen*—the last year of childhood.

In Coron's mind, the Master's voice was thin and high-pitched, half music, half whine. "Coron, I will tell you why you have failed me."

Listen!

"You have been weak. You have been lazy. The world outside is like a forest; the dead wood must be cut away. You must do the cutting."

The words Coron imagined were like a spider's silk, weaving around his mind, spinning a thick and clinging web.

The vision continued: "Adam must be brought here and sacrificed on this altar. All of The People must gather to see it. ALL MUST CELEBRATE HIS DEATH. You must hold the knife."

I will hold the knife.

Coron wallowed in madness.

"Yes, the old world is passing, and the new is coming. You have been weak and lazy. Now you must prove yourself worthy to be a king."

Yes, I was weak and lazy. Now I can be a king.

"You must do something that the world will see. You must announce your rule with terrible bursts of fire."

I know. I can see it. Those who oppose must die.

"You will rule as King of the World. All will look to you."

Yes, I am the center of the world.

"But, Coron, failure has its price. You must be free of distraction."

Yes, free of distraction. Yes.

"You must rid yourself of the woman who has distracted you. She has been sent as a temptation."

Marcia. Yes, Master, she is a temptation. I will extinguish her.

"You must not love anyone but me."

I know. I must love you more than I love myself.

SO WHY HAVE YOU BEEN THINKING OF A WOMAN'S LOVE?

Master, you are the one who will make me king.

KILL THOSE WHO DISTRACT AND OPPOSE.

Master, please don't leave me.

THINK ONLY OF ME.

Yes, you.

ME.

Us.

YOU.

Me.

Coron felt that a thousand blades of thick black pain were closing in on him, cutting and tearing.

He fell to the ground, exhausted, and was swallowed up by unconsciousness.

21

WEDNESDAY, OCTOBER 30, 2013

Adam woke up. *A gun resting on bones,* he thought. *I have killed twice.* He saw the flash of a gun and the glint of a knife.

The gun and the bones had remained hidden throughout the night, but it was inevitable that sooner or later the black boot of a fireman would nudge the charred evidence.

"Sir, I've found something," shouted a yellow hat to the white hat. "I think you should look at this." The fireman had been clambering over fallen ceiling beams in what used to be the kitchen, hosing down the very last of the embers.

They both swore. The man in charge muttered, "What the hell is going on here?" It was definitely a body.

Three hours later police were on the scene and the area was being photographed and meticulously picked apart. Soon, a gun was found. Later, another.

"What the hell happened here?" said the policewoman in charge of examining the scene. "It looks like these were in the boy's bedroom."

It was nearly midday.

About eleven o'clock, after a late breakfast and a deluge of comfort from Megan's parents that made Adam feel awkward, Mr. and Mrs. James said that they had to go out for a couple of hours.

Adam and Megan sat in the kitchen, heads resting in hands.

"There were lots of police there, Meg, I could see them. It's only a matter of time," Adam said.

"Adam. Listen. We need to bring this to an end now. You haven't done anything wrong. It's all *self-defense*. You're thirteen. You need to be kept safe." She looked right at him and produced the hint of a smile. "Look, *I* want you kept safe."

"I hear you," Adam groaned.

"You've been really brave and I think you're great, but now I just want life to go back to normal. Let's finish these drinks and then tell the police." At that point the doorbell rang.

Megan and Adam walked together, downcast despite their resolution. But it was not the police. Rachel, Asa and Leo stood at the door.

"Oh-my-God," said Rachel. "You're lucky to be alive."

Little do you know, thought Adam.

Rachel hugged Adam, more with her shoulders than the rest of her body. Then Leo took over with a right-handed clasp around the back of Adam's neck. Asa stood before Adam for a second and then the boys hugged tightly. They leaped back, surprised and embarrassed.

"I hope everything's cool now," said Asa, bouncing up and down slightly in an attempt to distance himself from this show of emotion.

"Yeah. Cool."

They sat around the kitchen table, and Adam gave a heavily edited version of events, glancing now and again at Megan, who knew the full story. All sorts of questions were fired in and answered with varying degrees of honesty.

Then, at nearly one o'clock, the doorbell rang and two indistinct blue figures could be seen outside.

"Guys, I think you should go," said Adam, his face drained of color.

Desperate to stay but clearly displaced, the three edged past two police officers, a man and a woman.

"Are you Adam?" the woman said. She leaned down slightly, trying to look unthreatening.

"Yes."

Megan stood very close. "And I'm Megan, his friend."

"We need to talk to you, Adam. We need to know some things about the fire."

Megan's parents were striding up the path behind the police.

"Officer? Is there a problem?" said Megan's mum, immediately fearing bad news from the hospital.

"We need to talk to Adam about the fire. Perhaps we could all take a ride down to the station and have a chat?" It wasn't a question, of course.

Mr. and Mrs. James frowned slightly at Adam.

Adam looked at Megan. "I think that would be a good idea."

Megan's mum was keen to take control. "Right, we'll come with you and act in the place of your parents. Megan, you stay here and we'll be back soon."

"No," Megan said immediately. "I'm coming with you."

The four of them followed behind the police car to the station. Megan's cell phone sat unanswered in her bedside drawer.

Chief Inspector Hatfield was standing on the steps to meet them. "I am so sorry about this, but we need to ask Adam some questions."

Inside, things were more formal. "We know that Adam's parents, unfortunately, are in hospital, so we hope that you, Mrs. James, can act as the *appropriate adult*."

Things moved quickly. It was as if Adam was sliding down ice, unable to stop himself. Bland questions came first, but Adam's answers soon led to the intruders, and then the gun. Chief Inspector Hatfield didn't seem interested in the intruders. Adam was the one who had killed. The words *then I pulled the trigger* made Megan's mum gasp. Adam stopped himself from saying *twice*.

After a second or two, Hatfield asked, "How many times?" His eyes narrowed as he looked at Adam.

He hates me, Adam thought. *He thinks I'm a wicked criminal.* "Twice," he mumbled.

Another gasp from Megan's mum.

It was as if the police already knew all the answers. Then more questions came about the gun.

"Have you used it on anyone else?"

"Who told you how to use it?"

Then: "We found another gun."

And: "Did you shoot your father?"

Adam felt the full influence of panic. "No. There was this man. And that's not all..." He decided to explain everything, even about the festival.

But at exactly that moment Chief Inspector Hatfield decided to pause. "I think we should let Adam have a break before we continue. Mrs. James, Adam is going to have to be remanded in custody, so I'd like to keep him in a room while we adjourn."

Mrs. James looked at the floor. "Don't worry, Adam. I'll see what we can do."

Don't worry, Adam repeated in his mind. The words were like fingernails scratching down a blackboard.

Remanded in custody meant that Adam was put in what amounted to a cell. He stared at the chipped walls and the metal letter box set at eye level within the door. After about ten minutes, Chief Inspector Hatfield returned to him with a different policewoman.

"Adam. This is a serious offense, and we have to take you to a different place for questioning. Mr. and Mrs. James and your friend Megan have to travel separately. As you know, you *are* under arrest."

Adam was depressed rather than upset. He still hadn't had a chance to explain things. When he did, it would all be okay. At least he was safe from the lunatics.

Passing a number of adults who looked away or glanced down, Adam was escorted out and into Chief Inspector Hatfield's car.

He sat in the back with the policewoman. She looked friendly, about his mother's age.

"The station is some distance from here, but you'll be fine. Try to relax."

Adam pushed himself back in the seat.

"You're next to Officer Wright," said the chief inspector. "But you can call her Marcia."

Chief Inspector Hatfield started to drive.

22

Megan again insisted that she stay.

This time her mother was less sympathetic. "Why don't you go home and meet Adam later at the hospital?" Then, quieter: "Supposing he's allowed to see his parents."

"When Adam explains he'll be a hero," Megan said. "You should have more faith in him."

"Megan!" her mother barked. "Your father and I should have cooled this . . . this . . . *relationship* with Adam weeks ago."

"We're just friends! Don't be so stupid." Megan glared, then stalked out, chased by her father, with her mother's parting shout—"How dare you!"—receding into the distance.

Megan's cell phone sat at home, dull black, unlit, unattended.

Adam breathed out slowly, gazing at cars lining up in the opposite direction. Adam only knew the name of one other London police station—Paddington Green, where terrorists were taken—so thought that his situation must be serious if he had to be transferred.

"Which station is it we're going to?" he said to Chief Inspector Hatfield.

"Oh, one outside London that deals with minors."

Adam noticed a sign for Brent Cross, which he knew was just by the M1, the main road heading north.

"Is it far?"

The woman next to him said, "It's a bit of a journey, so just relax."

Somewhere in the back of Adam's mind a flicker of concern was briefly lit, but then he closed his eyes and tried to imagine that he was somewhere, anywhere else.

Mr. James drove Megan home in aggressive silence. Worry and anger weighed heavily inside her. She leaped out as soon as the car stopped and stood impatiently by the front door.

"Megan, I've never known you like this," her father said.

"No?"

As soon as the front door was open she ran to her room, slammed the door and fell onto her bed.

Lying on her left elbow, Megan could see what remained of Adam's house. It looked like a blackened shipwreck: wooden beams poked skywards; rubble lapped round the edges. A handful of police and fire officers drifted around. Yellow tape swam in the breeze.

Megan felt her head start to spin. She looked at her clock. Nearly five.

Adam opened his eyes. The car had slowed nearly to a stop. Through the windshield he saw the back of a large green truck.

"How far now?" he said.

"Just a junction or two," said the woman.

Adam could see fields to the left and right. "Will I be able to see my parents today?"

"Perhaps. If you're good," she said.

If you're good.

The flicker of concern grew.

"Where is this police station?"

Chief Inspector Hatfield looked in the mirror at Adam. "As I said, *Adam*, it's not far."

If you're good. That sounded odd. *Where are we?*

The green truck was pulling away and they were gaining speed, moving into the outside lane. A sign whisked past: Services One Mile.

"I need the toilet. Can we stop?"

Adam glanced at the clock: 5:13 p.m. It was getting late.

Megan wondered what was happening with Adam. She looked at her bedside clock: 5:13 p.m.

She remembered her phone and reached into her bedside drawer. She switched it on. The name of the cell phone provider appeared, then a screen full of icons. Just as she was about to key in her mother's number, it pinged several times. Two texts were from Rachel, one from the cell phone company, one from her friend Karen and one from an unknown number. It was the last message that caught her eye. It started: "Tell Adam."

She scrolled down. Thirteen words.

"Tell Adam that Hatfield is evil. Don't trust him. Ask for another officer."

No name, no explanation. Evil? Not "bad": *evil.*

The car sped past the services.

"I *said* that we need to stop," spat Adam. "Please pull over now."

"Don't worry, we'll be there soon," said the woman, Marcia.

"Stop this bloody car—now!"

"Shut the hell up. Sit still, keep quiet. Marcia, keep him settled," said the chief inspector.

She reached out.

"This isn't right. I want to get out now. Get your hands off me."

The car sped up: eighty miles per hour.

Eighty-five miles per hour.

The chief inspector laughed. "You're welcome to open the door and get out any time you like."

Ninety miles per hour.

Marcia looked quite different now. Intimidating, crafty, sly. "Keep quiet and I won't have to hurt you."

The road was clearer and the car hurtled on.

"Mum, where's Adam?"

"The police have taken him off to investigate something. He's with the same policeman, the nice one who was doing the interview."

"Mum, he's in dreadful danger."

"Don't be silly again, Megan. The police will look after him."

Chief Inspector Hatfield flashed his lights and the car in front pulled into the middle lane. Adam could tell that they were traveling much faster than normal: the cars around them were probably going eighty and they were being overtaken with ease, each one making a zipping sound as it was passed.

Adam saw a blur that was the crash barrier.

"I'm calm. You can slow down now," he said, pushing forward slightly. "Really. I'm calm. See?"

Adam wriggled so that he was leaning between the front seats. He could see the speedometer on the far side. Ninety miles per hour. "I'll be good."

His hand slipped across the back seat toward the policewoman.

"I'm calm."

He unclicked Marcia's seat belt.

Immediately Adam thrashed out wildly, beating at both adults: he felt his right leg and arm make contact with Marcia. But it was his left arm that he concentrated on. From his position behind the passenger's seat, it was that arm he swung four times at Hatfield.

Adam's first strike had the benefit of surprise: it caught the driver in the eye and made the car swerve and ride against the central barrier in a cloud of sparks. There was a crunch and a high-pitched squeak. The side mirror was beaten off and clattered into a van driving behind them. The car rattled and shook.

Adam struck again, hitting jaw—too low. The car swerved back—Hatfield overcompensating, trying to keep at least one hand on the wheel—and edged into the middle lane. A motorcycle braked sharply.

Adam's right hand flailed at Marcia, his right foot stamped and kicked.

The third time Adam struck, his palm opened, nothing more than a slap. But with his thumb against Hatfield's ear, he dug a finger into his eye. Desperation made Adam's hand rigid like iron.

Both hands briefly left the steering wheel.

Adam no longer cared what happened: his fear was a bubble that hid him from logic and judgement.

The car veered to the left, crossing two lanes, and then careened back to the middle. Other drivers braked and honked.

As Hatfield turned, Adam struck a fourth time, grabbing hold of his throat. *They want to kill me!*

Chief Inspector Hatfield struggled to keep his right hand on the steering wheel. His foot hit the brake.

Marcia shouted something.

Time slowed.

Then the car began to drift slowly to the left, toward a truck parked on the hard shoulder.

Slowly, ever so slowly...

the car began to spin...

slowly....

Just for a second, less than a second, Hatfield completely lost control of the car.

And

And

And

SMASH.

part three

23

The impact was sudden. A jolt came first, then noise, then silence. The car had spun more than once and thumped into the rear of a trailer.

Metal crunched against metal; glass exploded into the car.

Adam had seen the red expanse race toward them. What first seemed slow and balletic had suddenly rushed to a *thump* and *smash*. Adam was lifted up out of his seat, and his seat belt dug into his shoulder. Marcia was thrown hard into the ceiling and door.

She died instantly, the investigators said later. No seat belt. At the impact speed of sixty-seven miles per hour she was more likely to die than to live.

Chief Inspector Hatfield, seated on the side of the impact, was probably saved by turning toward Adam, but his right shoulder and leg had been badly bruised, and blood dribbled from a head wound. Cuts on the right side of his face looked like an angry game of tic-tac-toe.

Adam couldn't hear anything. Outside he saw a blurred world full of stationary cars and people approaching silently, like lunar explorers.

A man and a woman rushed to Adam's door. "There's a kid

in here." Then they saw Marcia beyond him. Quieter: "Oh no. I think his mother's dead."

Suddenly noise and clarity returned to Adam. "I want to get out," he mumbled. "Get me out."

Chief Inspector Hatfield moaned and flopped an arm toward Adam. "Stop him. Help me out. Help me."

Gas started to fall onto the tarmac, just a drop or two at first, then a steady trickle.

"Get them out!" someone shouted. But the doors would not open.

Smoke and steam rose from the hood.

A man leaned in through the passenger window. Hatfield was already dragging himself across and was hauled out. Adam put his arms up and was halfway through his window. He wished that his body wasn't so floppy.

Underneath the car, gas started to snake toward the tiny sparks that dropped from the engine.

"Son, you're going to be fine," a man's voice said. Adam was shaken; scratches and bruises covered him, but adrenaline still ran in torrents. He stood up, tottering at first, but then, with his legs further apart, more steadily.

Voices came at him:

"You're in shock, lad. You should sit down."

"Keep him away from the car."

"His mother's in there."

Hatfield was laid on the ground. Adam could hear him saying the words *police* and *stop*, but in his civilian clothes the man looked like a delirious and anxious father.

Fire again tried to reach Adam. One little spark hit the thin finger of gasoline, and the line of flames started heading back toward the gas tank.

Hatfield, still on the ground, stretched his arm across the highway. "Fire—there will be a fire."

Adam edged away from the car.

There was a panicked flurry of activity; requests and warnings were shouted with concern and sometimes excitement; three people appeared with fire extinguishers and sprayed the car, unevenly but effectively.

All attention was on the immediate entertainment.

Adam looked across to the other lane. Traffic crawled past, faces turned toward the drama. Free theater.

He staggered toward the barrier that ran down the median.

"Are you okay?" asked a woman, wandering over.

"Yes, yes. I need some air, that's all," said Adam.

In the distance a siren wailed. People looked down the lines of vehicles to see a police car threading its way toward the scene, followed by an ambulance. Another distraction.

Adam sat on the central crash barrier. Further along he could see it had buckled and was surrounded by small pieces of debris, but here it was smooth and cool to his touch. As more people came forward Adam could see the scene becoming confused, individuals growing more interested in the event and less in the specifics of helping.

Another woman perched next to him and said, "Are you okay?"

"Yes, I just want to sit away from what has happened, quietly. Please let me go over there." Adam nodded toward the far side of the highway, across the opposite lane, away from the accident. "Please."

People rarely refuse children's requests. They usually help kids in trouble. Anxious, she glanced over at the crashed car, but who was she to stop the boy? She only made a half-hearted effort.

Pushing her arm away, Adam quickly dragged himself over the barrier, then lurched between the traffic edging south, the direction he had traveled from.

Chief Inspector Hatfield turned to look for Adam. He sat up, wincing. "Adam? Where is Adam?" he asked.

"Who?"

He thought for a second, cunning slipping into his mind. "My son. I want my son brought here."

Someone spotted Adam on the opposite lane. He was being hooted at by cars, then a bus obscured him from view.

"Help me up," said Hatfield. "Help me up *now*." He shuffled forward like a drunk. "I want that boy back here!"

Adam glanced back after the coach had passed, still standing between two lines of crawling traffic. He could see Hatfield rising and pointing.

A red Nissan Micra passed in front of Adam as he reached the very far side of the road. Six lanes separated him from Hatfield now, but their eyes still met through the traffic and the crowd.

"Get that boy!" screamed Hatfield. Thoughts of what Coron would do were beginning to well up in his mind, half formed, but preceded by acute desperation coated in fear. "He is not my son. I am a police officer." Hatfield poked around inside his jacket and pulled out ID, waving it vigorously in front of those around him.

A police car and an ambulance were stopping nearby.

Adam stared back as a tractor-trailer began to rumble past, the cab pulling a long white tank bearing a skull-and-crossbones symbol. He was hidden for a few seconds.

Hatfield shouted at the police officers who leaped from their car. "I am Chief Inspector Hatfield. Get that boy, now!"

The police looked across the lanes of traffic as the white trailer with its hazardous-chemicals symbol left their line of sight.

Adam wasn't there.

"He's over there somewhere. Check the trees. Call for support. Anything. I need that boy caught." Panic's bony fingers clawed at Hatfield's insides as he hobbled forward, staring up and down the highway for any sign of Adam.

"Adam!" he shouted. "Adam! Adam! Adam!"

The ambulance crew looked around from their place by the crumpled car and one of them went across to Hatfield. "Sir..."

The police officers ran, leaping in front of the cars and running up the bank. Small trees dotted the area, but Adam wasn't behind any of them. They reached the top of the slope. On the far side was a field scattered with cows.

"This is stupid," said one. "He can't be there. He must be on this bank. You go left and I'll go right."

Hatfield hobbled toward the center of the road, brushing off the paramedics trying to stop him.

After running for a couple of hundred yards in either direction, the policemen on the bank turned to the chief inspector, shrugged and held up their hands in a gesture of defeat. The boy had disappeared.

"Adam!" cried Hatfield uselessly into the pale sky.

Meanwhile, Adam was crouched down, grimacing as he clung to the back of the white tractor-trailer cab, as the road whistled past at fifty miles per hour. He held on to two thin strips of metal with stiff fingers, his legs vibrating between two precarious footholds. He was cold and felt faint.

Immediately behind him was a tanker full of something dangerous. But he was steadily leaving the real danger behind.

Chief Inspector Hatfield made three calls. The first was to the Old School House. Then he called the cell phone of a very senior police officer. Finally he spoke to his police station.

24

After about fifteen minutes the truck carrying Adam angled off the highway and slowed. A number of other long vehicles came into view. Adam found that he had seized up in one position. Then, as the driver dropped to the ground on one side, Adam did the same on the other, holding his back like an old man.

He ran to the trees beyond the parked trucks. The area was bleak, damp, metallically cold, lifeless. The trailers were obstinate weights dragged by aggressive engines. Drivers left their cabs in a hurry and returned reluctantly, wandering past oily puddles and soggy plastic bags. Adam felt a loneliness that he had never experienced before. The world had gone wrong.

In the distance sirens passed.

Adam sighed and held his head in his hands. It was dark. He had no money and no phone. He wished that he had taken some of the money from the shed. Just a tenner would have made all the difference. He had no ticket for London, no food, and only the clothes he stood up in: jeans and a blue Superdry top, the only suitable things that could be found that morning. The morning—so long ago, and things had seemed bad then.

Continuing the journey in the same way he had escaped the accident was not an option. Though he was desperate enough to take the risk, he could easily fall off and certainly would be spotted when the truck reached London. People would point. The police would be called.

He could steal something. Money? Adam didn't worry about whether this was right or wrong; suspected of murder, and at risk of abduction, what was a little bit of theft? *And I once felt bad about taking a packet of Toxic Waste from Mr. Rawley's Corner Shop*, thought Adam wryly.

Food from Dumpsters? Adam feared he would have to get used to that. Scavenging was the future until...until...*until when?*

He gazed into the distance as another bus pulled in, spitting out its crowd of passengers.

His mind turned over as he watched: each bus, regardless of the company, followed the same pattern. Tickets were rarely checked when people got back on. Children's tickets were *never* checked.

Adam had to move quickly; he had heard somewhere that criminals had to move fast after a crime. Or was that the police?

In the bathroom Adam noticed that most of his injuries were hidden by clothing, though his hands were grazed and dirty. He had a large bruise on his right shoulder and one on his right thigh. There were three cuts on his face, the worst just below his mouth. He dabbed at it but it still leaked blood. He shoved clean tissues into his pockets.

Others in the bathroom gave Adam wary stares. Although he was only thirteen, he seemed to provoke fear rather than concern.

Only one man, a burly truck driver, spoke: "You need to be more careful, son."

Adam wandered outside toward the busses, past CCTV surveillance.

At the same time, a police car, blue lights flashing, was heading down the highway to check the service station. It had taken the police twenty-five minutes to widen their search.

Adam saw that one bus was about to leave. The driver was

standing in front of the vehicle, drawing on a cigarette. An old lady was asking him something. "All right, my dear, I'll get it for you," the man rasped, then went to the low side door where the luggage was stored.

Adam saw his chance. He walked forward, head down, straight on to the coach and down the aisle. Those who saw Adam didn't notice him. A mother was feeding her daughter a cheese-and-pickle sandwich; a university student was searching for something on an iPod; an old man with a tie was engrossed in a *Daily Mail* article.

The siren was closer now, pulling into the service station.

Adam slumped into his seat near the back of the bus as the driver threw away his cigarette butt and clambered back on board.

"All here?" the driver asked, being friendly. He was nearly at the end of his journey.

"Yes," came the collective dull response.

"Anyone here who shouldn't be? Anyone forgotten?"

"No," said with slightly more enthusiasm.

Police officers strode into the service station as the coach pulled out.

Adam saw the clock outside Victoria Station: 8:47 p.m. Hunger ate at him, but he dismissed it, looking instead at a man sitting at the side of the pavement with a cardboard sign in front of him: Homeless and in Need of Help.

Adam understood that he was in the same position. He started approaching people, "Can you spare some change so I can get home?"

Six of the first twelve pedestrians ignored Adam; the other six said "No" (aggressively, with stares) or "Sorry" (sympathetically, but with similar stares).

He persisted. "Can you spare some change so I can get home?"

The thirteenth person stopped as if he had been expecting the question. He was a young man with glasses and rosy cheeks. He gave Adam the smile of one bubbling with contentment and mild amusement. "Yes, I can spare some change. It's my responsibility to *give*; it's *your* responsibility to *use it wisely*." He reached into his pocket. "Please take this as well. God bless you." He handed Adam a small leaflet entitled *Jesus Saves* and a fiver.

Five pounds! Adam had always dismissed a fiver as barely sufficient for popcorn and Coke at the cinema, but now it seemed like riches.

He immediately bought a cheeseburger and caught a bus that crawled through the packed streets of London toward Trafalgar Square. He looked at the people surrounding him and sighed; they seemed to have so little to worry about.

Buses passed Trafalgar Square monotonously, pulse after pulse, full of solemn travelers: thousands of people and a misty night to get lost in. The twinkling city lights were wrapped in gray.

A bus stopped; a child stepped off and dashed across the road as the green man flashed. Brown hair, slim, wearing a blue top.

Two policemen saw. "Hello," one said. "I think we've found our boy." The other spoke quickly into his radio as they broke into a run. They put out their hands to slow the traffic and crossed toward the lions and Nelson's Column.

The suspect walked quickly across the square.

"Let's get him." They darted forward and grabbed, forcing the child to the ground. There was no resistance.

"Adam Grant?"

"No, I'm not Adam *anyone*," came a girl's voice. "You've got *real* problems if you can't tell boys from girls."

She was a girl of about thirteen.

"Sorry," one of the policemen said, helping her to her feet. "Very sorry."

Then back on the radio: "False alarm. False alarm."

*　*　*

Adam threw a piece of gravel at the window. It made a sharp tapping sound and then another as it fell down onto a watering can. He huffed. *Damn. Come on.* He threw again, making more of a clunk than a ping. There was movement inside the room, and the curtain twitched. Next time the stone ricocheted off the window inches from a peering face. Adam waved his arms silently, vigorously.

Asa appeared at the window. "Adam?" He knew somehow that this was an occasion that required whispers.

"Look. I can't explain. I need your phone."

"Have the police let you go?"

"I'm not with the police." It was the best half-truth that Adam could come up with; it wasn't *actually* a lie. "Asa—I really need your phone."

"Why? Rachel and I have been doing a bit of texting."

Adam had to advance quickly to proper lies.

"I need to contact the hospital about my parents. My mum is *seriously* hurt. My dad might *die.* Megan's parents won't let me call." *Hospital* and *seriously* and *die* were words that hung in the air. Adam whispered and lied on: "I'll hand it back in a few minutes," he said.

Once Adam had the phone, he ran.

Megan's phone buzzed and she blearily picked it up. She had left it on in case another anonymous message arrived, but Asa's name was on the screen.

She pulled the phone under her covers and hissed, "Asa, it's eleven thirty. Why are you ringing me?"

"Meg. It's Adam. Listen. You've probably heard what's happened, or a version of it." He didn't pause, except to get a breath. "Hatfield was going to kill me, Meg. If I'm seen, I'm finished. I'll be handed over to the police, or worse, to Hatfield. Tomorrow night I'll try to find the boy who saved me and my parents. But until then I need to lie low. I need to rest and have something to eat and drink." He paused. "I don't have a choice."

"Oh God," said Megan. There was a pause. She felt that she was standing with her hand on a door, weighing up whether to enter, gathering the strength to make a decision. She knew that a lot of trouble lay behind the door, and that she would have to leave her parents behind. Whatever she did could change her life.

The pause grew into silence. There was a buzz and a hiss on the connection. Then she spoke. And she never wavered, right until the end. "Okay, Adam. How can I help?"

"I need some things." Adam listed three items. "And this is where I'll be hiding. . . ."

Megan's eyes widened as Adam explained.

As soon as they agreed where and when to meet, the connection was cut. The phone went dead. Megan tried to call back, but it went straight to voicemail: "Hi, this is Asa. I'm busy, probably with girls, so leave me a message. . . ."

Adam looked at Asa's phone. The battery was dead. *Sod it.*

There was a knock on Megan's door and her father walked in. "Megan?" her father said. "Megan, are you on the phone?"

A shaft of light illuminated Megan's bed, Megan, and the phone. She looked embarrassed. "I'm really sorry, Dad. It was Asa." She showed him the evidence on the screen. "He's having problems with Rachel. You know . . ."

Her dad took the phone, shaking his head, and said, "With everything else that's going on, the last thing we need is you girls and boys messing around together."

Megan's alarm sang under her covers and she was dragged from anxious dreams. She had set her alarm for 1:54 a.m.

Adam slept fitfully in the shed. He couldn't seem to get beyond the first chamber of sleep into the deep caverns that lay beyond. Every tap and rustle made him sit up, fiercely awake, and grab the shears he intended to use as a weapon.

Something clattered far in the distance, perhaps a cat on corrugated iron. Adam tightened his grip on the shears. He looked at his watch: 1:56 a.m.

Megan put on her nightgown, slid a backpack from under her bed and tiptoed downstairs—softly, slowly, secretly. Then, in the hallway downstairs, a sudden whirring and two solemn *bong*s from the clock: 2:00 a.m. The time they had arranged to meet.

Moonlight, shining through a tree, scribbled a pattern on the kitchen floor. No need for a flashlight.

She turned the key in the back door and froze. All quiet upstairs. Slowly, she opened the door; slowly, she went through and eased it shut.

Megan's father woke.

Adam unlocked the shed as Megan rustled down her garden and through the bushes.

Her father saw an empty bed. "Megan?" Worry edged into the fringes of his mind.

Adam saw Megan scamper past the shed window. The door opened. "Meg, I don't know what I'd do without you," he said as he weighed the backpack in his hand.

Megan smiled faintly. "Be careful. I don't trust the guy you're going to. He's not *normal*."

"This whole thing isn't *normal*, Meg. I'll try to get in touch somehow."

Megan's father went downstairs and stood next to the clock. "Megan?"

At the same time, Megan put her hand on Adam's shoulder. "Don't laugh, but I want you to take something." She pulled out a red wristband bearing the words *London 2012*. "It reminds me of the day we went to the cycling. I loved that day."

Adam still remembered flags and cheering, then their picnic, tearing cheese sticks in two and sharing pork pies. He remembered playing Frisbee and Asa singing a song from *South Park*.

Megan's father reached the kitchen door. "Megan?" His worry was maturing into panic.

"Oh, Meg. I don't know what I'd do without you." Adam's hand was shaking as he put it on Megan's arm. He felt so self-conscious, even embarrassed.

He put the wristband on and smiled.

Megan's mother dashed down the stairs: "Megan?"

Her father stepped outside: "Meggie? Megan?"

"Oh no," said Megan. "Hide!" She closed the shed door and stood in Adam's garden as her mother and father appeared through the bushes.

"Megan!" her mother said. "My God, Megan, what on earth are you doing?"

Megan looked toward Adam's old house. "Sorry, Mum. Sorry, Dad. I just had to come and have a look."

"Meggie, Meggie," her mother said. "You are being stupid. You must never leave the house at night again."

"Okay." Megan's parents saw her look at Adam's house, with its charred brick and fallen roof beams. The one place she did *not* glance toward was the shed, where Adam now hid, barely five paces away.

25

Coron strode up to Dorm Thirteen. Urgent, excited.

Asp was no longer there. She had used the gun.

Coron pushed a button to the right of the door, then used a key. A wild-eyed man in his early twenties scampered to the far end of the cell, terrified. Otherwise, the room was empty apart from a light sunk into the ceiling, small circular grilles in three of the walls, a bottle of water and a plate of food.

"I am *instructed* to be here," said Coron, "but you have *chosen*. You said you wanted to join us and then you wanted to leave. It isn't like that. This is a commitment that you must be trained into. Isn't it?"

The man didn't know if the answer was yes or no. "I don't—"

"Now, let me tell you something. I have done wrong myself. You see, I was told to kill a woman. Marcia was her name. And I was slow. I was wrong. I was weak." Tears leaked from Coron's eyes. "And the Master killed her himself."

For Coron, the unseen hand of the Master was everywhere. For Coron, the car didn't crash because Hatfield lost control; it crashed because the Master willed it. The Master, although a figment of Coron's imagination, dominated his entire thinking.

The man pushed himself farther back against the wall.

"And it is worse. The Master used *Adam* as his angel of

death," Coron whispered, glancing behind him to see if anyone was there. "Shhh. I'll tell you a secret. Perhaps the Master wanted to use him. I can't let the Master down again. I have failed to bring Adam here for his sacrifice. I must be punished."

The man was confused. "You? Punished?"

"Oh yes. I want you to understand that even I must be punished." Then, kneeling close, Coron whispered something else.

The man dragged his knees close and tried to hide his face behind his hands. "Please, no..." The crying began, as it usually did.

"Yes," Coron said. "I must suffer too, you see. We will suffer together." *I will suffer for my weakness,* thought Coron. *I will suffer badly.*

"And after we have endured our punishment together, we will consider what else is going to happen to you."

Little more than ten miles away from the Old School House, several police vehicles were parked on a small country lane next to a hill partially covered by large white tents. A line of officers walked through the field, gazing at the flinty ground in front of them, searching for evidence.

One of the white tents covered the area where Python lay, knife projecting at a right angle from the center of his chest, the body returned on Coron's orders so that Hatfield could pin the blame on Adam. Rain had smudged footprints back to mud.

Two other officers stood talking, looking down toward the nearby fields where Rock Harvest had been held. "The body must have been here since the festival, not very well hidden, but undiscovered somehow. The knife was left in, can you believe? We might be able to get a print."

A photographer was documenting the scene, each click of the camera underlining the severity of Adam's situation.

"And the suspect is the same child who shot the boy and set fire to his own house?"

"Yep. The boy had confessed to Hatfield, who was driving

up here to investigate. Then the boy went crazy and caused the crash."

Both officers shook their heads. Most of the time child criminals knew nothing beyond the dreadful world they inhabited. "Weird. And this boy comes from what seems to be a good home." The officer saw a man in a suit approaching. "Look out."

"This is a right bloody mess," said the chief superintendent. "I'm going on the six o'clock news before it's all over tomorrow's papers. I'll put out a description of the boy. Thirteen years old. *Bugger it.*"

"Do we have any idea where he is, sir?" one of the policemen asked.

"Vanished into thin bloody air. But he won't be able to stay invisible for long."

Just under one hundred miles to the south, five people, two of them policewomen, sat around the table in Megan's kitchen.

"I *said* that I don't know if he's in London," repeated Megan. "I have no idea where he would go, or what he would do, or who would help him."

In each case Megan lied.

"We know that you're telling the truth," her mother said, "but we need you to *think*. We just want to find Adam before he kills someone else."

Megan was thinking—thinking hard about how not to give anything away. "Is Mr. Hatfield going to get involved again?" she said.

One of the police officers spoke, moving her gaze from Megan to her parents and back again: "The chief inspector is keen to get back to work as soon as possible. We've heard what you've been saying about him, but he is a very experienced man, one of the best we have."

Then the other officer said, "Are you sure there's nothing else you can tell us?"

They think I'm just a silly infatuated kid protecting Adam, thought Megan. "No. There's nothing more I can say."

Less than 200 yards away from Megan, Adam was lying behind a locked shed door, wearing a pale gray hoodie from Megan's wardrobe. Tiny flecks of cereal and a half-empty bottle of tap water were just out of sight of the window.

£1,000, taken from a Quality Street tin, was in Adam's pocket.

Megan concentrated hard on not glancing toward the shed when talking to the police, but when she returned to her bedroom afterward, she allowed herself a glance at the small patch of roof visible through the bushes.

Adam stayed there until just after midnight.

26

FRIDAY, NOVEMBER 1, 2013

Adam knew where he had to go: the boy had said that he would be where they went through the water. That could only mean one place: the ponds, where they had once managed to escape him.

Paradise Fields wasn't far—just down a few streets, past a row of shops, and then across Park Avenue—but it was far from heavenly at night. Most of it was ominously dark, and tramps retreated there after a day in the center of London, but Adam welcomed the company of anyone else, especially those who had no sympathy for the police. *My world is upside down,* he thought.

By using the path that ran between houses, Adam managed to avoid one street entirely, and the next two were deserted. Most houses were dark and quiet, but the erratic blue glimmer of television screens still came from one or two upper windows.

The shops were closed and shuttered like eyes that refused to watch Adam. In the day it was a pleasant area that was being invaded by smart coffee shops, but at night it was steely, cold, drab and bleak. And exposed.

Adam walked quickly, then ran as he reached the main road, dashing in front of a taxi coming one way and a night bus the other. He didn't stop until he was wrapped in the darkness of the park.

Adam listened. He could hear drunken shouting in the

distance, but no one responding. A dog was barking. A tree creaked. Nothing else. *If some of the people here knew I had £1,000 on me, I'd be attacked in seconds,* Adam thought. He felt around the backpack for the flashlight.

As Adam neared the ponds it was too dark to see, and he had to put the torch on. The beam immediately lit up a man lying across a bench.

"Go 'way. Clear off!" Adam heard a couple of threats and ran on, into the bushes now, stumbling and bumping, until he reached the point where Megan and he had left the pond just over a fortnight ago. There was no one there.

Of course he won't be here, Adam thought. *He can't sit here 24–7 waiting for me to turn up.* He risked a quick flick of the flashlight.

No one.

Trees, pond, bushes, cans, plastic bags.

A waste of time.

Then, realization.

Wrapped around one of the branches was a tatty plastic bag, but it was the word printed on it that caught Adam's eye. *Silverstone*—the British Grand Prix. It was his big trip of the year, a boys' day out with his dad.

Images of his parents burst from the back of his mind: metal hospital beds with wheels, equipment that bleeped and hummed, pale skin, closed eyes. He forced himself to think of them sitting in the garden, smiling, before everything happened. But this vision fragmented away and was replaced by an anonymous hospital room.

Masking the flashlight with his hand, Adam went to the bag. There wasn't much inside, if anything.

He found half a postcard, folded over, and sixty pence, the cost of a telephone call.

Adam shone the flashlight quickly. The words *Greetings from Falmouth* and a picture of a headland and half a beach sprang out of the night.

Un-bloody-believable. They had stayed in Falmouth when visiting Cornwall in July. Adam turned the card over. Another burst of light. "Look inside the box you used when she lost her phone."

Adam thought. *She* must be Megan—Megan had lost her phone a few weeks ago. He remembered the day: everyone had been unsympathetic, saying that it was a crappy phone anyway. Megan had only realized because they were late and Adam had left his phone in his locker at school. So they had to use a phone box, one of the old red ones, for the first time ever. It was on the far side of the park by the war memorial.

Adam moved quickly. His head was buzzing. This guy must have been watching them for *months.*

Adam tried not to use the flashlight, but sometimes had to switch it on, its beam leaping up and down as he ran. He went as fast as possible, wary of anyone waiting to grab him. Despite being a good cross-country runner, he was out of breath when he reached the path behind the telephone box.

A bus and a few cars trundled lazily past. Adam found them vaguely threatening, imagining people looking at him from the windows, or getting out and pursuing him like zombies in a tacky horror film. He darted into the old-fashioned red telephone box, struggling to pull the door closed behind him.

The area around the phone was colorfully decorated with ads for girls, as well as three cards for taxis, one for furniture repairs and one for home removals.

Adam looked lower down: more girls of all shapes and sizes. Then a phone number next to the initials ATG & MEJ. Adam's and Megan's initials.

Adam rang the number.

"It's me."

"Stay there. I'll be on a bike."

The line went dead. Adam imagined himself riding away on a bicycle's handlebars. Then there was a tap at the window of the phone box. Adam would have preferred to see a gang of brutal robbers with knives rather than the two young policemen who stood there, a police car behind them.

"Can we have a word with you, lad?"

Adam looked through the glass. These were not aging coppers he could outrun; they were young and tough and probably much faster than him.

"And can we have your name, please?"

Adam couldn't think of a convincing lie. He *must* get better at lying. "Jim," he mumbled. *Jim. How idiotic.*

The policemen looked at one another. One of them turned his back and spoke into his radio. Adam clearly heard his real name along with a lot of jargon.

"I'm just going home." *What an idiot. This is it. Arrest. Prison. Or death.*

One policeman opened the door but kept Adam trapped inside the phone box; the other returned and asked, "Are you Adam Grant?"

"I have money. Lots of it. Just let me go." Adam pulled out a handful of notes.

The policemen didn't even look at the money. "You're coming with us."

Adam saw a motorcycle pull up at the curb. It wasn't a powerful machine, little more than a scooter, but it would seat two people. A seventeen-year-old boy stepped off, carrying one helmet and wearing another.

"Sorry, mate," came a muffled voice. "This kid's my brother."

"Please stand back, sir," said the policeman who had been on his radio. "We have reason to believe this boy is wanted."

From inside the helmet came another attempt: "No way! This squirt is always running about at night, but he's all right."

More words went into the radio and some came back, one of which sounded like *Hatfield.* There was something about injuries. Adam bore clear evidence of facial wounds from the car accident.

"Sir," the policeman said to the older boy, "you're welcome

to follow us to the station, but the boy must be brought in for questioning."

In an instant of blurred action, Simon swung the spare helmet into the policeman's cheek, knocking him backward, then sending him to the ground with a kick to the chest.

The other officer stepped forward, and Adam wriggled out of the phone box. He dashed toward the bike, grabbing the helmet as he passed. As Simon backed away the policeman reached out, but Simon twisted him around, dragged his feet from under him and thrust him to the pavement.

Simon ran across, threw a leg over the bike, kicked down and pulled away in a mist of exhaust, Adam clinging on the back.

The policemen could only watch.

A radio appeal went out immediately and was heard by a police officer sitting at a red light as the bike passed. "That's that one they've just mentioned," the driver said, looking at the bike and hearing its squealing engine.

Accelerator down. Lights on. Radio contact. Other cars were being called in.

Simon wound past a traffic island and went the wrong way up a road, then down side streets, angling left and right. But he couldn't escape: there was more than one car in pursuit now, and the bike didn't have enough power.

"Hold on," he shouted.

Adam pushed his knees close to the bike and wrapped his arms around Simon. He realized that the road they were on would lead them back to Paradise Fields, but Simon didn't slow as the turn came. From three hundred yards behind, the nearest police car saw the bike disappear into the park.

Trees and benches whistled past Adam as they sped down the main path, and then—with the lights off—across the field, dancing dots of light in the distance edging closer and closer. They went past the bathrooms and sundial, then, to Adam's amazement, when the road was at last in view, Simon cut the engine.

Adam could only hear the whistling of tires as the bike

drifted out of the park and squeaked across the empty road. Then they went down some steps at the side of a house; Adam bumped in and out of his seat, struggling to stay in place. Exhausted, he was hauled off the back.

Simon wheeled the bike, quietly, into a corner and covered it with a tatty sheet.

Adam was about to speak, but Simon put his finger to his lips, shook his head and beckoned Adam to follow him behind the houses.

Three minutes and five houses later, Adam was led through a rotten and scuffed back door. He didn't know whether he was more worried about the uncertainty that lay ahead of him or the threat that pursued him. *Is this a trick?*

The hall and stairway were dirty and undecorated. The carpet was ripped and threadbare in places, and brown wallpaper hung in patches that vaguely resembled continents. The door on the first floor was open, laughter spilling out into the hallway, and Adam smelt a sweet odor that he didn't recognize. Loud heavy metal music thumped from another room.

At the top of four flights of stairs they reached a plain brown door. Perhaps he would be grabbed and tortured to death? Dreadful images cartwheeled through his fatigued mind.

Simon opened the door; Adam hesitated.

"Look," whispered Simon in a low monotone, "you'll be free to leave at any time. D'you really think that if I wanted to kill you, I couldn't have done it already?"

Adam gave a tiny nod and followed Simon inside.

The flat had high ceilings, with crown moldings and fireplaces that betrayed it as part of a once-grand house that had clearly fallen into disrepair and become a squat. There was a chipped table in the middle of the room and two or three chairs with the flowery patterns that old people liked. Simon led him past an old, chain-operated toilet and into a stale bedroom. Being with Simon in the flat seemed odd, but being in a bedroom was creepy, even for Adam.

"Look," started Adam, hesitating again. "I don't..."

"Please be sensible. Why is this room more dangerous that that one? I could have knocked you out and dragged you in here."

Simon then prodded open a door in the ceiling, and a rickety metal ladder slid down. It looked as if it led to the loft. "We're going up here." He sounded so much older than seventeen.

I must be mad, thought Adam, as he followed Simon up the creaking metal steps. Simon pulled the ladder up behind them, and in one movement the door snapped shut, leaving the room in complete darkness. Adam closed his eyes for an instant and the same blackness remained. He could hear Simon moving away from him.

What was I thinking? I've been so stupid.

27

Coron went down the stairs again and knelt before the Master.

For a time he almost dreamed. Ghostly men with no eyes and bony faces swarmed around a rusting tractor on a farm. Dark clouds crackled overhead. Birds swept down on a scarecrow, pecking open its stomach. Worms poured out of the ground, which became a sea of wriggling slime.

Then a train appeared, carrying children with no faces, and standing at the back of the final car was the Master.

Coron's eyes flicked open. The Master was before him. Immediately. Completely. Screeching and thumping continued in his ears, and somewhere in the distance he thought he heard crying.

"I enjoyed your punishment." The Master's voice was pitched even higher than before, almost feminine. "I was with you. I am always with you."

"Master, I empty myself for you." Coron bowed his head. He heard screeching in one ear, thumping in the other.

The Master continued. "Adam is the one. The old rebellious god is using him to torment us."

The Master was coming closer to Coron, alongside him; whispering, touching.

"He must be sacrificed publicly. Just as two thousand years

ago there was a sacrifice on a hill." Lips were tickling Coron's ear. "He must be taken to the highest point in the city and sacrificed. And at that moment our reign will begin."

Coron imagined the sharp triangular building pointing up into the sky and Adam, arms outstretched, secured at the very top. A glass shard piercing the Imposter for all to see.

The Master was seeping into Coron. Dark blood pulsed through him, turning arteries and veins to cracked black channels.

"I am here." The voice was in Coron's right ear.

"I am here." The voice was in Coron's left ear.

Then behind.

Then deep inside his chest. "I am here." Then: "Find Adam. Bring him to us. Sacrifice him on the eve of our new kingdom."

"Yes, I will please us," Coron murmured.

He felt tugging and twitching as the Master left him.

A wispy swirl drifted away across the room and noise became louder: he imagined helicopters and roaring and the clanging of pipes. Louder and louder.

He saw the train again. This time there were faces.

No—one face.

Again and again and again, looking out from every car: Adam.

Seagulls screeched as they curved and twisted above a vast port. Below them, thousands of containers were chaotically colorful. In the distance, nearly thirty cranes pecked at the boxes, lifting them from huge ships.

Each container was twenty feet long and eight feet wide; three-and-a-half million of them passed through the port of Felixstowe every year.

Like ants with leaves, trucks shuffled and shunted the containers. On one vehicle was a blue one, plain apart from letters and numbers at the top right. It was one container among millions.

Inside this particular box, wooden crates were stacked from floor to ceiling. To a seagull, this was a tiny detail; there were thousands of wooden crates and thousands of containers in a port with a quayside over a mile long.

Two of these wooden crates had traveled over eleven thousand miles, criss-crossing the globe on their way to Felixstowe, now nearly at the end of their journey.

The crates were destined for a remote address about a hundred miles north of London.

Clunk. The container was dropped into place.

Open the crate, open the crate, the seagulls seemed to cry.

Inside the crates were explosives and the other materials necessary for bomb making. There was enough material here to destroy a small town—or the center of a large city.

28

Simon switched on the light, a single bare bulb.

Adam saw they were in a large loft space. He struggled to take in his surroundings. The room had been half boarded over, but in places he saw thin yellow insulation fiber between the roof beams. His eye was drawn to a small table in the middle of the space, scattered with a handful of papers and maps. Everything there was to do with Adam. His stomach suddenly felt very empty. "What the hell is going on? This is *bloody* wrong," he muttered.

There was one other small desk with a laptop on it, and a thin mattress and duvet. Next to that was a small fridge, several bottles of water and a bucket with a sealed top.

"You're a *weirdo.*"

Simon spoke. "You can leave when you like, but hear me out."

Adam pulled his fingers into fists, though more for show than anything. Odd though it was, Adam didn't feel scared. This boy looked so *normal.* He was adult height and broad across the shoulders, but could have passed for a sixth-former. Adam couldn't work it out. He couldn't make up any story that would explain what was going on. "This is seriously messed up."

"Okay. A drink? It's not poison," said Simon. He took a swig from the slightly creased plastic bottle and handed it to Adam. "You're in big danger."

"Really? I wouldn't have guessed," said Adam sarcastically.

"Possibly from you."

Simon laughed slightly, little more than a heavy exhale. "Sit down. We can go downstairs, but I'd rather be careful and stay up here. The building was taken over by squatters a few years ago, and they're still here. I met a couple of the guys downstairs when I was on the streets."

Adam leaned against a roof beam. "Maybe you should start with *your* name," he said.

"Simon. Let's forget my last name for a sec."

"And why do you keep on saving my life?" It was a serious question delivered without humor. Adam looked down. "Thanks, by the way."

Simon laughed properly, then leaned forward. "Adam, I'm just going to spit this out. It's bad and it's weird, but you're ready to hear it straight up."

Adam *was* ready. "My life has been turned to crap. My parents are nearly dead. I've killed, and nearly been killed. I want to know what's going on."

"Okay. Well, first things first: you're safe with me. There was a time I would have killed you and been rewarded for it— but don't panic, you're safe." Simon held his hands in a gesture intended to calm.

"I hope that's right."

"It is. Believe me, I'm in *almost* as much danger as you." Simon looked eager to throw his information in front of Adam. He moved about uneasily on his chair, as if he couldn't get comfortable. "I used to be in this group called The People. A cult. Weird, wacky nutters—I see that now. But I was four when my mum and dad joined, and I knew no different. Just imagine it: no TV, no Internet, nothing. I only found out about your world because I was sent out into it."

Adam put one hand on his forehead.

"Get ready, Adam. Please, *please* don't run when I say this."

Adam frowned and leaned forward, an involuntary suggestion of trust.

"I was sent out to kill. To kill boys. I did three, all born at midnight on millennium night, just like you."

Adam recoiled. "You! You've killed?" He almost said *like I have*. He tried to imagine this older boy killing, but couldn't.

"Yeah, me. And each day I'm attacked by the guilt." Simon thumped his hand into his upper chest. "The only way I can heal myself is by doing some good. By protecting you."

After a few seconds of tense silence, Adam nodded. His eyes went around the room as he thought. "But I wasn't—"

"Take it from me: the one accurate thing in all of this is your birthday." Simon took a very deep breath. "Look, however mad it sounds, this group, led by a guy called Coron, believes you're some sort of...a danger...the fourth in a series of great figures born two thousand years apart."

Adam shook his head, fascinated but despairing, mouth slightly open, eyes staring.

"It's all in a book written by Coron himself. It says that if you get to be a man—and according to him, that's when you're fourteen years old—you'll get your..." Simon shrugged as if he couldn't find the right word. "*Powers*, and be able to sort them out. I think they believe that you will reign in their place unless you're killed."

"They're insane."

"Yeah. I know that more than anyone. Coron sees things, hallucinates. And there's over a hundred of them in the cult, maybe more, including lots of kids, and people like..." He paused for an instant. "Chief Inspector Hatfield."

"What the...?" Adam didn't have the energy to finish the sentence. He thought about how he just wanted to be normal and hang out with Megan and Asa and Leo.

Simon continued, "I even helped them search for you; that's how I know who you are."

The story and his profound tiredness were smothering Adam. It was all so unreal.

"We're in this together. As far as I know, I'm the only person ever to leave The People and live. I first went on the streets, then found this place. We need to stay out of sight here until December. The date set for their 'kingdom' is January 1, 2014. They're bound to do something stupid involving guns, maybe even bombs."

Adam sometimes swore, but always on purpose. This time the word just slid out of him, more of a sound than a comment: "Shit."

"So we have a month to go, then we will call the police. If we wait, I think they can be caught red-handed. I know where their base is: a place called the Old School House. In the meantime we're going to stay here, in these few rooms, nearly all of the time."

Adam rubbed his eyes and struggled to make his words sound lighthearted: "Is that all?"

"Not quite. It does get worse."

"Simon, mate, it can't get any worse."

"My name is Simon Hatfield. That policeman—he's my father."

Adam spat the word out: "No!"

"Yes," Simon continued, "and the girl at the festival..."

Adam nodded slowly.

"She's my sister."

They stared at each other.

Adam said two words: "It's worse."

part four

29

TWENTY-FOUR DAYS LATER: MONDAY, NOVEMBER 25, 2013

Morning

Chief Inspector Hatfield stood before Coron, head slightly bowed as he spoke. "I know. I know. I *know*."

Coron sat back. "Be careful."

"I'm sorry." Then, quietly, "I am very sorry." Hatfield gesticulated with tight, frustrated hands. "There's still no trace of him. Someone is hiding him, I'm sure of it, and the girl must be the link. But I'm certain that he has made no *direct* attempt to find out about his parents—no letter, no call, nothing electronic. The girl, Megan, is being watched: she *never* meets him."

"I do hope that you are not making a basic mistake. The universe—our whole universe—hinges on the sacrifice of Adam. For your sake, I hope you're trying hard enough to find him."

Hatfield had explained repeatedly that all lines of inquiry were being investigated. Megan was being monitored closely. Her email, phone calls and Facebook were checked; they had even looked into possible intermediaries (Rachel? Leo? Asa? Her own parents?), but neither the police nor cult surveillance had found any evidence of her using anyone else to communicate with Adam. "We recovered the letter she posted yesterday. It was a card to an aunt in Toronto."

Coron closed his eyes in angry despair, then bellowed, "It's him! He *has* left the country."

"I feared so myself, my lord. But the Ontario police were quick to confirm that the woman exists. And the message was simply 'Love from all of us.' "

Coron thought. "Perhaps he is using a different form of communication? Something spiritual?" He shook his head. "No. The Master would not permit it now that the battle in heaven has been won."

"I'll redouble our efforts. We'll have three police officers and ten loyal members of The People watching her journey home this afternoon. If she drops anything or passes something to a third party, we'll certainly know."

Coron spoke to himself, almost in a trance. "Police interference has only managed to put her on her guard. She helped him that first night, and she is the one taking messages to his parents. The Master is right."

"My lord?"

Coron looked up. "The very fact that she is *not* looking for him betrays her."

Afternoon

A pace back from the window, Adam peered through binoculars and spoke to himself: "Here she is. Ah—yellow! She must have been to visit my parents."

Megan was walking her usual route home through Paradise Fields. Held against her chest was a yellow science folder.

It was on the fifth morning after Adam's disappearance that a figure in a hoodie had leaned forward as soon as Megan sat down on the bus and whispered, "He says thank you for the wristband. Before Rachel joins us, get off and meet me where he went the other night." Megan went there quickly. In a blur of efficient, grown-up conversation, a system was established: Megan would use school folders to display information as she walked home, around four o'clock, past the sundial near to the western entrance of the park. She laughed when Simon quoted Adam: "She'll like this arrangement; she treats those folders like pets."

The system had served them well for almost three weeks.

Her yellow science folder meant there was a message to be dropped into one of the bins near to the sundial, which was clearly visible from the top floor of 53 Park Avenue; her blue history folder meant all was well; her red one—English—meant there was trouble. Simon left urgent messages on the window ledge outside one of the cubicles in the nearby ladies' public lavatory, a tatty building thick with bushes on the far side. But he insisted this would only be every fourth day, and he would try to deter Adam from sending anything.

It was the yellow folder—a message!—that afternoon.

Simon was muttering about money. "We've got 481£ left, so we're in the clear. Only five days to go, then I think we'll tip off the police. If we lose our nerve and go sooner, they might not find anything, and we'll both end up in some sort of institution." He wasn't listening to Adam. They had been in one another's company for over three weeks. Three weeks during which every newspaper had carried daily news of the search for Adam.

Adam squinted and pushed the binoculars harder against his face. "She's wandering past. Now, where are you going to leave the message?"

Megan dared not look up at the tall houses that overlooked the park. How incredible! While the police followed up possible sightings everywhere from Cornwall to Scotland, Adam was here, right under their very noses.

Displaying the appropriate folder, knowing that she could be seen, felt like a full conversation. And it was easy to slide a message inside a wrapper or tissue and drop it into a bin, though she had done it only three times. Adam had sent two mildly confusing coded messages, both intended to reassure his family.

Megan had to be casual. Acting flustered was simply a matter of adding to what was already there, but pretending to be casual was difficult; hiding her anxiety took real effort. Despite the gray weather, there were quite a few people around, and she was wary of everyone. *Be casual!* she thought. A boy and his dad fed a squirrel; a jogger stretched on the step below the sundial; a middle-aged couple read the information about the rose garden. Other people were at the periphery of her consciousness. *Be casual!*

A message written inside a tissue explained that Adam's mum was out of the hospital and would be staying with her sister, and that his father was much better but still under observation. She was going to drop it into the bin under the oak tree, as if it was a natural and thoughtless act.

Adam put the binoculars down. He could still see the shrubs and rock garden around the sundial, as well as the field in the distance, where he had once fought Jake Taylor. "Si, there's more people today, and unless I'm going paranoid, they're watching Megan. Mate, stop me worrying."

Simon shuffled over. "Pass me the binocs." Black circles surrounded figures as he looked from person to person. "Oh my God. Turn on the phone!"

Five buttons were pressed:

Contacts

Meg

N

O

SEND

Megan ambled toward the bin and dabbed at her nose with the tissue.

"What's going on?" asked Adam.

"Bollocks. They're on to her. I know at least five of those people." Simon and Adam stood back from the window and crouched down, suddenly fearful that someone would look in their direction.

As Megan approached the bin she felt her phone buzz. A one-word message: "NO."

She frowned and quickly deleted it. Then she put the tissue in her pocket and walked on. But she couldn't help glancing around and hurrying.

Evening

Coron and twelve others sat around a table. Jugs of water were set in the middle, papers and pens scattered around. It looked like a business meeting.

A woman was speaking very deliberately, often glancing at Coron. "So I suggest that we place one here"—she tapped at a large card—"and here"—another tap—"as well as in the places already established. These last two can be placed there on the day by anyone. The area isn't restricted."

The man at the head of the table nodded. This was taken as general approval.

"The explosion here," she added, pointing, "will be the biggest. Because of its location, the device can only be placed by servants Hatfield and Cook."

The man at the head of the table picked at his hands. The scars itched sometimes, a reminder of his role. "The Master says that we can't concentrate on this because we have been slow to seize Adam. ADAM!"

Everyone looked down, except Viper, whose gaze never wavered from Coron's face.

Coron laid his hands on the table, as if to show that he was calm. "Lord Coron wants to know about the transmitter. The devices must set off everything *exactly* at once. *Exactly* at midnight."

Prompted by nervous glances, a young man, little more than twenty years old, spoke. "Yes, Lord Coron, we will have a range of over a mile. The transmitter will work well at the top of the building."

Coron stood up and went over to two large wooden crates. The meeting had started with everyone peering at the contents. "When we have the world's attention—and ADAM is sacrificed!—all will bow down to me, and to the Master."

Coron kicked the side of one of the crates. A significant cache of explosives sat inside, separated into about forty different packages. He reached down, picked out a number of the plastic-wrapped squares and placed them on the table.

"I want these to stay here; I have a special purpose for them. The rest are to be taken to the London house. We must knock down before we can build. We have been slow to see how powerful and imaginative the Master's ways are. Our devotion to the Master must be absolute."

Coron felt the Master welling up inside him, using him as a mouthpiece, his words tickling, enticing, enthralling. "One day you will be in glory. And not in some distant world, but real glory here on earth. Here, where pleasure is as real as flesh and blood. Pain teaches and punishes; glory rewards and electrifies. You are the chosen ones."

How lucky we are, they thought. *Millions—billions—of people on earth, and we are the chosen twelve. We are the ones in the same room as Lord Coron.*

"You are the twelve. One day you will sit on thrones ruling the world with me. And our time is near. The Master has shown me everything. His hand guided mine as we completed our book."

Coron closed his eyes for about thirty seconds. At these times the Master blended into him. They spoke as one. Inspired. Unique.

"I want you to bring the girl Megan here. She knows where

the Imposter is. But she will not tell willingly; pain will be needed to draw the information from her."

"We will make it so, Lord Coron."

"And the Traitor, who has been helping the boy—we will break him into a million pieces."

Break him, they thought. *Yes. We will destroy him.*

"And leave two people in the park. Adam is nearby. Somehow he was there today. TODAY! ADAM! We have traced the text that she received, and it was made from the cell tower that is near the park. The girl was being watched, and she knew it."

Coron looked at Viper and smiled. *She is young,* he thought, *but she is the best of my disciples, even better than her father. How unlike her brother,* the Traitor.

Coron spoke in a flurry of words. "We must thank the Master. We must thank him with a worthy sacrifice. Bring down the man from Dorm Thirteen."

30

Excitement about Adam's whereabouts did not dim in the month after his disappearance. On the playground Megan was often surrounded by other kids peppering her with questions, like journalists keen for a straight answer from a politician. Megan preferred interrogation by the police.

"Did you know he was going to kill people?"

"So you've no idea where he is then?"

"Has he sent you a message?"

"Did you think he was going to kill *you*?"

Megan looked at each of the excited faces surrounding her. She couldn't blame them for asking, and though it was irritating, it wasn't real peril, not of the sort that Adam faced. And it would have been much worse if they truly suspected she was in contact with him.

Mr. Sterling dawdled across to the group. "I am sure that Miss James has answered enough questions for today," he drawled. "And I need to cross-examine her again myself."

Walking in silence, Megan followed Mr. Sterling to his office door. He turned and frowned. "Can I help you?"

"You asked for me to come with you, sir."

"Oh, yes. I thought you might need a break from that nonsense. I have no intention of asking you anything." He smiled. "You wouldn't tell me anyway."

"But..." Megan started. "I..."

Mr. Sterling stood with his hands in his pockets. "I refuse to do a jigsaw when I don't have all the pieces. And I'm sure you have more of the pieces than anyone else." A rapid *clip-clip* sound was approaching down the corridor. He looked behind Megan and muttered, "Deny everything."

Megan frowned as Mrs. Tavistock appeared, dressed in a neat dark blue skirt and jacket. "Megan, I wondered if you wanted another chat?"

"Miss James was just saying how much she would have liked to have a word with you, but was worried about being late for the trip," Mr. Sterling said, closing his office door to stop the headmistress from peering inside.

Mrs. Tavistock puffed herself up slightly and spoke in the tones of an anxious grandmother. "Well, Megan, you know that I am always here if you need someone. I *really* understand what you are going through, dear."

Megan thought of Adam's impersonation of Mrs. Tavistock, widely held to be more like her than the real thing. "Yes, thank you. That's very kind," she said politely.

Mrs. Tavistock wondered how such a good girl had become involved with such a nasty boy.

Mr. Sterling looked at his watch. "That's it. I have to go. I'm part of this ordeal today. I hope there's something good to see."

Mrs. Tavistock snapped into a high-pitched rebuke. "Mr. Sterling. You shouldn't jest. It's the British Museum. The British Museum!"

The trip to the British Museum was seen by most at Gospel Oak Senior as an inevitable but mild torment, at best an opportunity to escape lessons and, hopefully, teachers. Leo and one or two others were secretly looking forward to it, but only the most committed nerd would have admitted such a thing.

During the journey, conversation had drifted from Adam's whereabouts and guilt on to either football (mainly the boys) or who fancied whom (a topic explored with equal enthusiasm by everyone).

Megan's class was given worksheets and sent to rooms full of Roman artifacts. Megan, Rachel, Asa and Leo immediately formed a unit.

"Right, Meg, you write it down for our group," said Asa, peering lazily into a display case. Then his face was alive with entertainment. "Holy crap! Have you seen this porn?" He was pointing at a 2,000-year-old silver cup depicting an adult scene.

"Asa, you're disgusting," said Rachel, with the tiniest flicker of a smile. "You've got a one-track mind."

Megan wandered over. "That's what you're interested in, is it?"

"You bet!" he chortled. "My parents wouldn't let me look at that sort of thing."

"I didn't know that was your sort of thing," said Megan, pausing just long enough. "They're both men."

Asa peered again at the cup. "Well. Nothing wrong with that." Then, nudging Rachel, "But I happen to prefer the female of the species."

People were staring.

It was then that Megan noticed the girl in the doorway. It was Cassie from the festival.

Viper, whom Megan still thought of as Cassie, was holding a small piece of paper, alternately tapping it against her chin and glancing at it. She slid it on top of a glass cabinet.

Megan strode across the room and collected the note. Viper retreated to the far end of the next gallery.

The message was blunt: "Follow me."

Megan looked round. Her mind spun: *What can go wrong? We're in the middle of London.*

Asa was pointing at other artifacts now, trying to locate the rude and amusing ones. Even Leo was joining in. Only Rachel saw Megan leave the room. She followed.

Viper stayed about twenty yards ahead of Megan as they wound their way toward the exit. Hundreds of people milled around. *I must be safe here,* thought Megan.

Just as Megan followed Viper, Rachel followed Megan—and it was Rachel that Mr. Sterling saw heading toward the door. The deputy head had positioned himself far away from the front line, where worksheets and ancient history did battle with thirteen-year-olds; he was by the exit, a packet of cigarettes tucked into his jacket pocket.

He followed, and the four parts of the chain were strung through the front door and outside. It was only as he left the building that Mr. Sterling saw Megan up ahead, approaching the street. He swore and started to run, already puffing by the time he passed Rachel.

Megan reached the road, which was busy but not wide. Cassie—Viper—stood on the other side. "Wait there," she said.

Mr. Sterling could see Megan standing on the pavement talking to a girl—not one of his kids, she wasn't in uniform—across the traffic. *I really* don't *have all the pieces,* he thought, as he saw a white van stop and the side door slide open a few inches in front of Megan. Mr. Sterling ran.

And someone from behind pushed Megan into the van.

Weight giving him momentum, Mr. Sterling threw himself in front of the closing van door and looked inside to see Megan held by a woman. A voice in his ear: "Get back. We are taking the girl."

"Bugger off. She's staying with me."

Megan struggled hopelessly. Viper climbed into the passenger seat and turned around.

Tourists wandered past, stared briefly, and quickly moved on.

Viper threatened him: "If you don't go, you're getting a bullet." Then slyly, "Look up, *sir.*" She was holding a pistol.

Sterling didn't think about being a hero. He didn't weigh up chances or consider options. The words just tumbled from him: "I'm not leaving this girl. Let her out."

Two seconds later there was the dull thud of a gun that has a silencer.

Megan screamed. Rachel and some passersby realized that something bad was happening.

Mr. Sterling was pushed from the van and the door slid shut. Despite a growing circle of blood beneath his left shoulder, he still tried to reach for the vehicle. "Let her go," he croaked from the curb.

Rachel stood on the pavement, shaking with confusion and horror. She didn't think to look at the license plate and hadn't noticed what the people had looked like. She ran back into the museum, shouting, "Help, somebody help!"

Inside the van Megan was grabbed tightly. She could feel the press of a gun and was unable to speak because of the hand clasped over her mouth.

Viper turned around. "I'm going to enjoy this," she said, smiling.

Megan was held hard against the floor in the back of the van as it jolted through London. Two adults pinned her down, but it was Viper's voice that taunted. "I am going to punish you if I have the chance. It's only right, given the way you've helped that boy. But I might show *some* mercy if you tell me where he has gone."

Megan could see Mr. Sterling's blood on the floor. A couple of trickles moved back and forth across the metal as the van twisted through the winding streets.

"I don't know where he is," mumbled Megan. She wanted to be brave, but her mind shuddered at the thought of dying so young.

"In that case, we might as well just kill you immediately," Viper said. Then she turned to the driver. "Move into that lane; it's going faster." And to Megan again, "Or we might wait, if you help us."

Megan pressed her lips together.

"We might even let you go."

Megan gradually regained her composure. If they were going to kill her, they would have done that already. She tried to blot out what was being said and listen for clues. They were certainly in heavy traffic, but that could be on any of the routes out of London. Soon they were going faster, with occasional twisting stops, probably traffic circles. Then they were at speed. *A highway?*

Megan could hear one half of a phone conversation about her unwillingness to explain where Adam was. Viper was agreeing with someone. Then she was chuckling.

After about twenty-five minutes, Viper turned around and spoke to the adults in the back. "Please do make her less comfortable about...now!" They were passing the place where Adam had caused Hatfield to crash.

Megan was lifted and pushed and jabbed.

Soon after, the van slowed and started winding through smaller roads. Eventually it came to a stop, and there were voices outside. Then, thirty seconds and about six hundred yards later, the side door opened.

Coron stood on the gravel. "Hello, Megan. My name is Coron. Welcome to our home." He put his hand on her shoulder and looked straight into her eyes. "Sooner or later, you are going to tell me where Adam is. Most people would feel awkward hurting you. But I am not like them."

31

FRIDAY, NOVEMBER 29, 2013

Adam's sleep was shattered in an instant. A shaft of sunlight had squeezed past the window blind and sparkled on his face. For a few seconds the world would not settle and make sense. *Where am I? What time is it?* Then the heavy weight of truth fell on him. He was still in Simon's flat. He had not stepped outside for four weeks.

He was lying on top of a duvet. Standing up, everything became blurred and liquid for a few seconds and blotches clouded his vision. His brow felt heavy with fatigue.

Enduring the confusion of light-headedness, Adam pulled open his bedroom door and saw Simon sitting at his computer. The television played in the background, something about government debt, then a noisy clip from parliament.

"What are you doing?" Adam yawned.

Simon picked up a subject they had discussed many times over the previous four weeks. "I'm looking again at that Google Street View image of the road outside the Old School House. I've seen that fence ten thousand times from the inside and four times from the outside. And one of those was when I escaped." He left unsaid that the other three times accompanied murder.

"Just call the police. You don't have to go there."

"I have to be *certain* that the police will find something

when we call them. What if the place is deserted? Or, worse, what if everything looks completely normal? I will have handed myself over and be a few fingerprints away from years and years in prison. You as well, possibly. I know that other murders took place, but I can't *prove* it. I don't even know where the bodies are buried." Simon used both hands to ruffle his own hair vigorously. "I just need to see enough, or at least to know that Coron is there. Then I'll call the police."

Adam tried again to convince Simon that he should join him. "I can't bear being stuck here. Even you go out sometimes. It's doing my head in! What if you're caught? It's been four weeks and there's another month to go before you think I'm safe." He flopped into a chair with as much force as possible. "And even then I might not be."

There was a picture of earthquake damage on the TV screen.

Simon had heard it all before. "The real danger is now, while you're thirteen. I didn't help you to have you walk right into Coron's hands. When the police see there's something bad going on at the Old School House, we can let them know the full story."

Adam was about to say that he had heard all *this* before when he froze. "Look!" he shouted, pointing at the screen. There was a picture of Megan and the single word *KIDNAPPED*.

He fumbled with the control, holding it the wrong way around. They heard a man's sober voice mention *teacher* and *shot* before the sound rose.

"...British Museum. If anyone saw a white Transit van or anyone acting suspiciously at the time, please contact the police."

"No! No!" The room closed in on Adam. He swore repeatedly about Coron and the situation, then turned to Simon, "I suppose she's at the place you're looking at."

"Possibly; I don't know. As you know, there's the London house—if *only* I knew where; she could be there." He pointed at Adam. "Let's not be stupid."

Anger tore through Adam, instantly, explosively. "It's my fault." He edged closer to Simon until he was under a foot away, shouting all the time, "How can I just sit here while she's with him? Eh?"

Simon stood up and walked across the room and back. "Listen. I've messed up. I've killed innocent people. It's different for you. You're *thirteen*, for God's sake. You're being stupid."

"And you're only seventeen, Si." Adam moved to even greater thunder: "Screw you! We're going together."

Simon knew that Adam would never give up. It was one of the things he liked about the younger boy. Simon pressed his left palm to his forehead and tried to disguise his admiration. "Okay. We'll go together. But when we know that they're there, or if we see anything odd, we'll call the police immediately. They'll have to arrest them all if Megan is in the house."

Adam nodded, excitement, optimism and fear mingling to produce a nervous smile. *This could be over soon,* he thought.

Simon didn't smile. "You are stupid. Brave, but stupid."

32

Coron was a tall, slim, athletic man, with a thin, even elongated, face. When he spoke, his voice wasn't at all the demonic growl that Megan expected. "I think you should thank those who have brought you here. Please say thank you." It was such a peculiar thing to say that Megan was unsure if he was being sarcastic or sincere.

Everyone waited. Megan said nothing. She found it difficult to stand and steadied herself against the van.

"Perhaps you were right, Viper. Perhaps we should take her upstairs straight away." Coron opened his palms, showing fresh and deep wounds. "Please say thank you."

Something about the scars told Megan to be compliant. "Thank you," she said, hating and regretting it immediately.

Coron continued, his voice slow and musical. "I *wonder* if you know where Adam is." He studied Megan's face as if trying to sense, or smell, the answer. "Yes, I think you do." He nodded. *Oh yes.* "I think you are a *clever* girl. You know that you will tell us eventually." Then, softly, but very much a threat: "Or I will have to damage you."

Megan wanted to protest, wanted to explain that she would never, *ever* cooperate. But she looked to the ground. Nothing would be gained by proud and foolish words that prompted a beating—or her death. Death. Ripples of fear spread through her stomach. When she thought of dying it was as if her insides were being shrunk.

Coron's eyes were like dark marbles. "I think we will give you one day to tell us. Then you can have a central role at our final Feast here. It is one of our great events. After that we are leaving for somewhere else, you see. Somewhere less..." Coron gestured at the buildings and fields around him, "...less open."

Megan wasn't sure if attending a meal was a threat. "Will you let me go?"

Coron laughed. "It is not up to me. The Master decides everything here." He continued, solemnly, "I would like you to join us." He meant it. "But in the short term your only hope is to tell us where Adam is. You see, that's the most important thing of all. He is the hinge on which all the events of the next few weeks depend." Coron looked at the others. "We will try gentle persuasion over the next day. Then the Feast."

Megan was taken to the second floor. Her room could easily have been part of a hotel and was certainly nothing like a prison. She immediately searched for something, anything, that could be of use. There was no phone, nothing sharp—not that Megan could have fought her way out—and the window was too high to jump from; besides, there were people outside. Megan had heard of stranded travelers reflecting the sun to call for help, but what with? And who would see? Or understand?

All too soon a knock came at the door, followed by Viper's voice. "Don't keep us waiting. There is something Lord Coron wants you to experience."

Megan emerged, now dressed in a blue-and-white striped dress that had been laid out on the bed for her. She hadn't wanted to change, but Viper had said that if she didn't they would rip her old clothes from her. She sensed it was a threat they would have carried out.

Thoughts of making a run for it disappeared when she saw

that Viper was accompanied by a large, silent, aggressive-looking man. They led Megan along a corridor, up a winding staircase, and then up a much smaller set of steps that turned twice at right angles. The walls were covered with brown paneled wood. It could have been a stately home. At the top of the final flight of stairs there was an open door.

The room was waiting, apparently empty. Step by step she edged closer to it.

Megan could see a number on the door: thirteen.

Dorm Thirteen. It was an empty, plain, windowless room, with a shiny wooden floor. Megan saw the three grilles in each of the walls and the single bright light.

Viper closed the door behind them. They were only a year or two apart, but she spoke as if she was an adult and Megan a child. "Here you are, little girl. This is where we put naughty people."

Megan walked the five paces to the far end, trying to work out the danger. Perhaps something nasty would drop from the ceiling.

Viper anticipated her thoughts.

"No, no, no. That's far too quick. This room gives you time to consider your errors. A lot of time."

She thumped the door.

The noise started. It was loud, too loud for Megan to block out by putting her hands over her ears, but not quite damagingly loud. The noises were unpredictable, sometimes ugly descriptions or horrible phrases, sometimes screaming or other jarring sounds, always over and over and over. Not on a loop; similar, but varied. Different voices, crying and shouting, persistent and piercing—over and over again. A jumble of nastiness.

Megan heard a loud passing train, a bell and hysterical laughter, then screaming. It abruptly stopped.

Megan thought that she could probably blot it out if she tried to think of pleasant things.

"Yes, everyone believes that at first," Viper said as if she had heard. "Would you like to stay and try?"

"No." The noise had already generated images that made Megan shudder.

"Of course, not all of those screams are pretend. Maybe yours will be recorded and added."

Megan felt her resolve breaking under the weight of her despair and fear. "You're sick in the head."

Viper opened the door. "You need to have some color thrust into that simple mind of yours. A little part of me hopes you won't tell us where Adam is. I would enjoy seeing you hurt."

"I don't *know* where he is." Megan felt that this was all unreal, a story that would end with *and it was all a dream.*

"Megan, Megan..." Viper put a hand on her shoulder and squeezed gently. "Lord Coron is a great leader. He is our shepherd. He needs to know where Adam is, for the good of everyone. And you will tell him before the end of tomorrow. Lord Coron will ensure that the Feast is a *special* occasion."

The word *special* sounded like a threat.

And, as if the mention of his name had summoned him, Coron appeared at the door. "This room is far more effective than you think. It's useful as a short punishment, of course, and most people can withstand the first day. It's the sleepless nights that break people down. After the third night, people will say anything for a few minutes' rest. After the fourth, they don't know what to say. It would work on you."

Megan wanted to run, but there was nowhere to run to. She was cornered prey.

"Unfortunately, we don't have time for this method. And I can't risk you getting confused. It's simplest if you just tell us where Adam is."

"I don't know."

One long breath later, Coron spoke again. "I feared and expected you would say that. The problem is that you don't understand us. But I understand you, Megan. I know that if I left you in here all night, you still wouldn't tell. No. You will sleep in your bed tonight. Safe and quiet. Viper, take her to her room. Feed her well. Make her comfortable."

Megan frowned. Surely they did not think that they could *charm* her into telling?

Viper put her arm around Megan's shoulder as they left, but it was shaken off. Then, just outside the room, Megan saw the large, threatening man holding the shoulders of a girl who looked about twelve. The girl stared at Megan, silently pleading.

Coron spoke when Megan was halfway down the first flight of stairs. "This is Peringuey. She is a good girl. An innocent. She will spend the night in Dorm Thirteen on your behalf."

Megan tried to turn, but Viper held her. "No. I'll do it. I'll stay. Put me in there."

Coron suddenly shouted, "Then tell us where ADAM is!"

Megan looked down, frozen by thought, then mouthed to Peringuey, "I'm so sorry."

Megan lay back on her bed and tried to force the experience from her mind. She was stubborn and resilient. Wasn't she?

But she couldn't stop thinking about the other girl. And Adam, and the Feast (what *was* that?) and her worried parents. And her own death. The thoughts dug deep into her mind like roots. She buried her head into her pillow and cried, grabbing handfuls of the soft duvet and pulling it tightly around her. Why were people like this? And, finally, the wail of utter desperation—*It's not fair*—which became an anxious groan.

Finally, fitfully, Megan fell into an uneven and thin sleep.

Megan slipped out of bed and crept across the room. She had heard the key turn last night and the door was still locked. The window was also bolted—she had considered smashing it with the bedside table, but flashlight beams had been wobbling about outside and she'd heard the occasional yelping of dogs; even if she'd broken out and somehow inched herself down, her situation was hopeless. And maybe they would kill her if she attempted to escape. If she tried, she would have to make sure she succeeded.

She thought of her parents and how they would be consumed with worry, rigid with tension, eyes full of tears. Then she thought of Adam. Surely by now her abduction would have made the news? Perhaps Adam would have seen it?

Then she thought of the other girl, guiltily: *I should have considered her first. She's suffering because of me.*

There was a knock at her door. A woman came in, with Viper behind her.

"I hope you slept well and had sweet dreams," said Viper.

"Go to hell," said Megan, the words spilling out before she had time to stop them or to craft a better insult.

Viper smiled as Megan seethed. "We have woken up grumpy. I hope that doesn't mean you're going to be awkward. Get dressed and come with me."

As they walked through the building, Megan realized there were lots of people around, including many she hadn't seen the day before. Heavy boxes were being moved, and with some urgency; it was like an evacuation before a storm. With all of this activity, could she slip away? Could she send a message?

Megan was led down a central hallway and into a room that resembled an office, except for a large painting above the fireplace of a dark angel emerging from a swirling cloud. Megan noticed a chilling normality about the room: a London *A–Z*, a guide to modern architecture, scissors, phone, briefcase.

Coron leaned against his desk. "Megan. Now that you have had a chance to reflect on the suffering that Peringuey is enduring because of you, perhaps you would like to stop it by telling us where Adam is?"

No. She couldn't say. They would kill him. At least the girl wouldn't die. "I don't know."

"You won't tell." Coron moved to the other side of his desk and gazed out onto a lawn and what appeared to be a summer house beyond. He spoke with his back turned. "I feared you would be stubborn. Let me be very clear." He turned around and put his hands together, steepling his fingers. "If you don't tell me by this evening, I will kill your parents."

"What?" Megan shouted and stared. "What?"

"I would kill a hundred parents if need be. A town. A city. More depends on finding Adam than you can imagine. I will do whatever it takes."

Despite everything, Megan still wondered if the threats were idle, an adult frightening a child. Maybe. But *her parents*? This was the worst possible nightmare. Whatever she did, someone would be hurt.

Perhaps saying where Adam was would be the lesser evil. At least he would be expecting trouble. Maybe he had moved. And he might have heard about her kidnap. At least she had until that evening and the Feast.

Coron nodded as he looked at Megan. "You will tell us at the Feast. Of that, I am certain."

Megan sat in her room and looked at her watch. Maybe she could drag out the seconds. Each nudge of the hand brought the possibility of rescue. But time dripped on, relentlessly ticking closer and closer to the Feast.

Occasionally Viper would come into the room to torment and threaten; once an old lady visited and explained about The People.

"I hope you will listen to what Lord Coron says," she said. "I wouldn't want you to miss out on what is going to happen. Once the boy has been sacrificed, we will guide the world. That is a great thing to be involved in. Perhaps you will join us."

Megan frowned and lowered her voice. "Can't you see that it's all wrong, that it's all mad? That killing is wrong? And Dorm Thirteen—you know that's torture?"

"Oh dear, what a strange thing to say. We are guided by the

Master and live well. No one steals here; we all walk around safely; and Dorm Thirteen helps those who are bad. Lord Coron wouldn't allow it to be used without good reason."

Much later, the door opened and Megan was given a new white dress and told to put it on. It was an hour until the Feast. "This is our final Feast in this house, Meggie," said Viper. "A very special occasion. The celebration begins at midnight; afterward we will leave this house to prepare for our new reign."

About thirty people sat around a table with Coron. They banged their knives and forks on the table and shouted, "Feast! Feast! Feast!"

Led by Viper, Megan walked in, her eyes drawn to two kneeling figures at the far end of the large room. It looked as if their hands were tied behind their backs. Between them was another table, but this one had a tablecloth. *No,* Megan thought, *not a tablecloth. An ALTAR cloth, like in a church.*

NO!

"Feast! Feast! Feast!"

Paintings hung on the walls, each one depicting sacrifice, and Megan saw words painted just below the ceiling: "I will deliver you into the hands of brutal men who are skillful to destroy. You shall be the fuel for the fire; your blood shall be in the midst of the land."

"Feast! Feast! Feast!"

Coron stood and the chanting stopped. The only noise was whimpering from the far end of the room.

Arms outstretched, Coron started. "The Master is here. He wants to feast on a worthy sacrifice. And there is no worthier sacrifice than a willing one."

I can't cope with this, thought Megan. *It's too horrible. I can't think.*

"The Master tells me that Adam will come as a willing sacrifice. And tonight, we may have a willing victim. Megan?"

The room spun slightly with confusion. Megan felt faint. "No. *No.*"

"Megan, you have a choice. Tell us where Adam is, or there will be a willing sacrifice."

"I'm not willing." Confusion. Spinning. So many smiling faces.

"If you don't tell us, it will be *your* will that these two people are sacrificed." Coron gestured toward the kneeling figures.

Megan shouted, "That's not willing. I don't want anyone to be hurt!"

"Then tell us! Tell us and your parents will live; tell us and these visitors will live."

A deathly and evil silence hung in the room.

"Tell us, and *you* will live!"

Tears filled Megan's eyes. The words formed in her mind: *He's in number 53, top flat.* She looked at the eager faces.

She pushed her lips together to stop any noise coming out. *He's in number 53, top flat.*

Smiling, grinning, smirking faces looked at her.

And Megan realized that whatever she said, they would not let her go. They could not let her wander away to the police. Adam would certainly die. Her parents? These people were capable of anything.

No. She would not tell. If need be, she thought, choking back tears, she would die as she had lived, trying to do the right thing. She . . .

At that moment she heard movement behind her, and a figure rushed straight to Coron. There was whispering.

Coron smiled and looked up. "People, the Master is a wonderful god. The boy Adam has been seen. I believe he is on his way here." Then he began to laugh. It wasn't a sound that came from his mouth alone, it bellowed from deep within him. "The Master is indeed God; he is perfection. Adam will be a willing sacrifice; he will surrender himself to us. And the Traitor will deliver himself for punishment. 'The Traitor will choose to place himself in Dorm Thirteen.' It is all written! Just as it is written that we will rule the world and the universe!" He walked toward Megan, who stepped back and nudged into two men. "If only you were not blind. One day all will serve the Master." The men held Megan tightly.

She started twisting and pulling, then Coron's nearness made her fight furiously to free herself. "Get away from me. Let me go...."

Someone appeared from behind her: Viper holding a cloth. It came closer, smelling strange. Sweet. It was pressed to Megan's face. She couldn't get free, though she kicked and wrestled. And her world tipped upside down and faded.

Megan fell to the floor.

33

Underneath a dripping tarpaulin, Simon's small motorcycle waited for the two of them. It was five doors away, across paved yards and small gardens behind houses. Now fully at ease with furtive behavior, Adam enjoyed the midnight drizzle on his face and drank in the damp autumn air.

Simon took the front wheel and Adam the back as they heaved the bike up the steps at the side of number 48. It was when Simon pushed it to the curb that the man standing directly opposite, like a sentry at the entrance to the park, suddenly noticed them. In the seconds before helmets went on, he clearly saw Adam with Hatfield's son. Wide-eyed, he hissed to someone behind, "Quickly!"

The moped groaned under the weight of two people as it pulled away. Simon saw a figure, arms flailing, in his rearview mirror, and used the throttle, urging the machine on as the man lunged. Fingertips just grazed the back of the seat, then the man fell, instantly unmoving, as the angry buzz of the motorcycle drifted off into the distance.

Another man came out from the shadows of the park and immediately phoned the Old School House; within ninety seconds, Coron had been informed of the sighting.

Adam dared not speak; he simply clung to Simon just as he had a few weeks earlier. They traveled mainly by side streets and then avoided the highway, even though this added over an hour to the journey. Simon stopped twice to consult the map, but he recognized the way as they neared the Old School House.

It was about 1:30 a.m. when Simon pulled off the main road onto a much smaller track running between trees. The mud was a slippery gruel that meant the bike had to be pushed for several hundred yards. Apart from trees gently rustling like a hushed audience waiting for the start of a play, there was utter silence.

After about twenty minutes, Adam could see the eastern boundary of the site. It took Simon five or six minutes to cut the wire topping a six-foot-high wall. Adam imagined running down the drive, helping Megan as cops streamed in, then hugging his parents while a grateful police force applauded.

He was thrust back to reality as Simon called down to him. He'd dragged himself onto the wall, and now put out a hand to pull Adam up. Together they sprang down to the other side.

Adam looked back up at the wall. There was no going back now. He could see the Old School House to his right. To his surprise, the building was bathed in a yellow glow, giving it the appearance of a country church eager to attract tourists. He expected lights to be shining away from the house, seeking him out. Instead, every light in the building was on.

Adam squinted; halfway up the front of the house he could see a large black smudge, insect-shaped, dangling like a spider. Fear scampered over him. He didn't want to draw the obvious conclusion. *No, it isn't a person. It can't be.*

"The lights are new," whispered Simon. "What is that dark thing?"

They edged closer to the house through thin woodland. Snaps and rustles were shouts and warnings. But sounds in the distance concerned Adam more: the barking of a dog, the ticking of an engine, the slamming of a door.

There definitely was something or someone on the face of the building. *No, not Megan, please. It can't be.* Adam was dizzy with fear. He took deep breaths to ease his nausea.

Then they saw a piece of cardboard nailed to a tree. There was writing on it: Sidewinder—Hurry. The cardboard was damp rather than sodden: it had not been there for long. Simon was pale. "That's me. Sidewinder."

"What?"

"All the kids have names of snakes; that was mine."

A few trees later, they saw another: Sidewinder—Help.

"They know we're coming," said Simon. "But they couldn't have known the route we would take. These signs must be everywhere."

Adam listened, his face and body rigid, and wondered if he would hear a bullet before it hit him. If he died, would he know about it? Or would the world just go black? Years of life, thousands of hours, millions of minutes ending in one unexpected second. Doubt poured into him. Was he right to have come?

Between the trees, they saw the black shape against the building: it was twisting slightly in the breeze, center stage in the lights. It was definitely a person.

And the tree they waited behind had another crude sign: Sidewinder—Quick!

Adam wanted to run. He now pictured himself running down the road away from the house, the thin rain cooling him as danger gradually disappeared pace by pace.

"We don't need to see any more," said Simon. "That's a body, and I'm calling the police." He pulled out his phone and dialed 999. The call shot from cell tower to cell tower, then onto wires, under roads and beneath buildings, until it rose through the floor under a desk into the headphones of an operator.

"Emergency. Which service?"

"Police," said Simon.

The line buzzed and Simon was asked to explain the nature of the emergency and give his details. "Something terrible has happened at the Old School House on the London Road. And I think Megan James is being held there."

"Please stay on the line...."

Simon was silent.

"Please stay on the line...."

But Simon had seen something. "No, no," he muttered, pointing.

"This is all wrong," said Adam. "Why the hell would they do this?" He could now see that the dangling figure was a young man. Dead. Thirty feet from the ground, arms stretched between two ropes. For a terrible moment Adam felt relief—it wasn't Megan!—but this was soon replaced by dark panic and horror. "Let's go back," he whispered. "Let's wait for help."

But Simon went closer still, silently, until he pushed Adam back behind a bush, out of direct sight of a surveillance camera on the corner of the building.

Adam was more afraid of the light than the dark. He had expected to be dodging spotlights and jumping from ditch to ditch. Perhaps The People were all hiding somewhere out here?

"I'm going in." Simon looked toward the building and pointed to an open doorway. There was a sign made from a large wooden board: "Sidewinder. You are needed inside to stop your sister's pain."

"No," hissed Adam. "No. Wait." Why were the police taking so long?

Without a word, Simon ran across the grass, the powerful lights forcing two shadows from him. The open doors led straight into some sort of conference room. Every light was on: four chandeliers and nine wall lamps. There was no one there. On the table he could see a large piece of paper covered in black capital letters.

Adam waited. Silence. He checked the bushes behind for a trap. Nothing. Still silence.

Suddenly Simon was shouting, an anxious wail. "Adam, Adam! Come here! NOW!"

Adam sprinted across the lawn and through the doors.

Simon was pointing at the table. "My sister is upstairs; Megan's in the summer house." He pulled open an inner door and was gone.

Adam noticed the sheet of paper: "Viper is in Dorm Thirteen. Time is running out. Megan is in the summer house. Adam—be quick."

"No, let's wait! This is *very* wrong." But Adam still dashed outside. Summer house? Yes, he could see a small timber building at the edge of the light.

Simon tore through the building, heading for the main stairs. He took them two or three at a time, throwing open two doors, and then went up the final flight. The door at the top was closed. Locked. He could hear noises from inside: screaming, rattling, bells.

Help Me was written underneath the Dorm Thirteen label.

NO! He smashed against the door.

It is written that the Traitor will choose to place himself in Dorm Thirteen. Coron laughed. The Master laughed. They both laughed.

Simon hurled himself against the door again. Desperation flooded through him.

Adam ran across the lawn toward the summer house. As he reached the stone path he slipped, both feet disappearing from under him. Ignoring his bleeding leg, he sprang up and hobbled on.

Further seconds slipped away as he peered through the dark windows. He tugged at the door: locked, but it looked flimsy.

Adam smashed once, twice at the door.

Simon smashed one more time. The door splintered. Screams tore through Dorm Thirteen. Were they Viper's?

Adam and Simon both shoulder-barged their doors. Adam's door cracked open; Simon's door shattered.

In the gloom, Adam could just about see a large envelope with his name on it. Stepping back into the light, he tore it open. Inside was a cell phone and a plan of the grounds and surrounding roads, including a snaking dotted line. There was a large letter C at the end of the line and a message: "Use the phone." He swore, then stepped back and looked up at the main building. *Simon?*

Simon stepped into the room. He saw thirteen packets of putty-like explosives and two words scrawled on the wall: The Traitor.

He saw the wires that led back to . . .

The door.

Simon heard a bleep.

He raised his hands in a futile attempt to shield himself. There was an enormous explosion.

The building was ripped apart. Adam saw flames leap from the upper windows and through the roof like angry dragons. Then there was a second blast, lower down, that smashed through the ground floor, cracking windows and blowing out doors. Adam was more than a hundred and fifty yards away, but the heat was searing and specks of masonry rained onto the ground around him, pinging off the path. The entire building was alive with flame that leaped with malevolent triumph.

Adam looked at the phone. He pressed the green button: one number was there. As the flames roared around him, he pressed it again.

He couldn't hear the voice at the far end properly, so shouted over it. "Listen to me! I'm going to kill you!"

34

SATURDAY, NOVEMBER 30, 2013

Megan emerged from a confused blend of reality and dreams. She could vaguely recall people shouting at her as she struggled.

Shadowy traces of two nightmares hung in her mind. In one she was crowd-surfing above jabbing arms, roughly pushed from person to person as bands of light and dark passed overhead. In the other, sweet-smelling hands tried to suffocate her but then broke into a thousand droplets of water.

Her feeling of being bound up had not been a dream: she was wrapped in a sleeping bag on a bare mattress. Although she could not raise her head more than a few inches without pain tightening around her skull, she noticed that the room was windowless and lit by a single bulb. Voices passed outside like distant sirens.

Megan closed her eyes and disappeared into a shallow sleep filled with a kaleidoscope of leering, blurred faces. She didn't know if it was minutes or hours later when Viper gradually emerged from the misty colors. "Yes?" Megan muttered.

"I thought you were dead," sneered Viper as she shook Megan. "Eat and drink. And there's no point looking for a way out: there isn't one." Someone had placed water and a bowl of plain pasta on a bedside table. Megan noticed that she was now free to move. Between forced mouthfuls, she pressed at a bruise on her forehead.

Coron rushed in, flanked by two men in black gowns.

"Megan, we are seeing history unfold before our eyes. In seconds Adam will call. In minutes he will hand himself over as a willing sacrifice."

Megan uttered the desperate words of the fraught captive: "Please let me go."

"Megan, if only you understood the glory of tonight. And in one month, just one month, the world will be turned on its axis. This city and then the whole world will be torn away from its rotten foundations."

Megan realized that she would never in any way be able to reason with these people. Her hopelessness paralyzed her.

The phone rang. She could hear Adam shouting. Coron spoke: "*Adam*. Be careful who you threaten. You should consider the health of your parents first. And speak to Megan."

The phone was passed over.

Megan spoke quickly, "Adam, it's terrible—they're going to kill our parents and me! I'm in London somewhere, and they want you, and I think they're going to blow something up—"

Coron prised the phone from her hands and Viper restrained her. Megan struggled desperately, like a drowning woman clawing at the surface.

Adam listened in silence as the building crackled and fizzed in front of him.

The words he heard were methodical, calm, unnervingly precise: "This is Coron. Now listen to me. Look at the map."

Adam stared, his hands shaking with anger and frustration.

"There's a car at letter C. I will give you fifteen minutes to get there. When you're inside it, use this phone, and I will not kill Megan or your mother and father. Following the path marked by the dotted line will mean that you avoid the main entrance and anyone coming to investigate the fire." Flames were leaping thirty or forty feet in the air now.

"Let Megan go first."

"No, I think not. You get in the car, call from there and then I'll let her go. She can walk away, and go can home."

"I HATE YOU, YOU BASTARD." Fury and terror strangled Adam's ability to think. He shouted, "Okay!" It was hopeless. This man was organized and had people and resources. Adam wanted to scream senselessly, wanted to get help, but the one person who could help him had just been murdered. Where the hell were the police? He pressed the red button and the phone went dead. Adam looked at the map. The dotted line directed him around the back of the building and through what must be another exit.

Viper turned to Megan. "Don't get your hopes up. You're not going anywhere."

Megan was open-mouthed. "But you said... You—you lied!" She cried, hopelessly, pathetically, "ADAM!"

Coron smiled. "Yes. You helped deceive Adam, like Eve deceiving man in the Garden of Eden. And you may have to deceive him again. If you refuse, Viper will have the privilege of offering you as a sacrifice."

Flames from the Old School House reflected in Adam's eyes as he looked at the map. The letter C marked the location of the car Coron had sent. The car: the capital, Coron, capture. But Adam could not believe that it would all end with his own death.

He ran along the gravel path indicated by the dots on the map, flecks of the burning building catching on his coat. Initially lit flame-orange, the path disappeared behind some trees into increasing gloom, and Adam was in near darkness when he reached a metal gate.

A short, muddy path led to a country lane. The letter C was very near if he turned left.

The car: the capital, Coron, capture.

I won't end up a hero, he thought. *I'll be trapped and killed. I won't be able to beat up a lot of adults and rappel from a window. I'm going to have to do things differently.*

Adam turned right and sped up. He raced past a couple wearing the ill-matching attire of people who have dressed quickly in the night. They hurried down the road, presumably from the farmhouse he could see lit up in the distance. The man was on his cell phone, saying something about seeing flames behind the trees. When Adam neared, they shouted, "Hey! You! Stop!"

Adam sprinted on without looking back, soon into woodland, keeping the glow from the burning building behind him. The uneven path, strewn with puddles, was taking him in more or less the right direction. Branches clawed at him and he slipped more than once, but no one seemed to follow, though it was hard to tell.

Just as the glow from the building was fading, he saw a flash of fire engine lights in the distance to his right and soon came to the path where they'd left the motorcycle.

Adam heard an urgent buzzing and saw the screen of Coron's phone glowing through his jeans. He realized that there was no going back now.

Coron spoke as soon as Adam answered: *"Adam,* you don't seem to have arrived. Megan is getting worried. Your parents would be worried, if only they knew."

"Listen to me," said Adam. "We're going to do things my way."

Coron shouted so loudly that Adam pulled the phone away from his ear. "No! You listen to me! People are going to get hurt if you don't get into that car right now."

"Go to hell. *You* listen to *me!*"

Coron was furious, stumbling over his words. "Listen to Megan—go on, go on, listen!"

Adam could hear someone saying his name and a sharp

scream, but much of it was lost in the wind. With tears in his eyes, he bit his lower lip. "No," he said, his face full of agony. "No. I will hand myself over, but not your way. You bring Megan somewhere public, like Trafalgar Square, and I will let you take me if you release her. Otherwise I'll hide until the New Year. I'll hide until I'm fourteen and then come and kill you."

Coron, possessed by anger, grabbed Megan's throat.

Adam didn't pause: "Trafalgar Square, tomorrow—that is today, Saturday—five p.m., by the lions. Let Megan go and I'll leave with you."

There was silence at the far end of the phone, apart from Megan's gurgled crying. Eventually Coron spoke, "All right. You have just over twelve hours. Every hour, I will keep Megan uncomfortable. Would you like to hear some more?"

If Adam spoke he couldn't hear Megan. "I'll be there if you leave my parents alone and don't hurt Megan." His mind was whirring.

"You are playing a dangerous game, Adam," said Coron.

The drizzle was turning to rain. Adam pushed the scooter to the main road and used the key that was hidden under the seat. He was used to bicycles, but it was an unsteady transition to something motor-driven, so he wobbled his way through a village speckled with street lamps, nearly falling off by a church and again by a white building that was probably a pub. After that, he found that more speed kept him upright.

Soon he found an arrow-straight, blue-black road and a sign that promised London.

35

Trafalgar Square is dominated by four lions and one tall pillar, Nelson's Column. As Adam's bus drove past, he could see Megan standing in the space behind this famous landmark, with Coron's arm around her shoulder, shadowy figures in the early-evening gloom. A woman was taking a photograph of them. Megan was grimacing; they looked like patient father and quarrelsome daughter.

Adam pulled his hoody around his cheeks. How many of the people he could see were Coron's People? Adam couldn't distinguish between the suspicious behavior of an extreme cult and the unpredictable movements of tourists.

Adam looked at his watch, partially hidden by the red wristband that Megan had given him. It was still only 4:45 p.m., so he went on a couple of stops and then passed again on a bus going the other way. This time he could see people talking into cell phones. Kids clambered on the stone lions and chased pigeons. *Does everyone belong to Coron?* Adam wondered.

The woman across the aisle was staring in his direction, probably; the man in front turned around twice. *What about them?*

The bus crawled to the next stop. Adam stayed on, changed again and came back a third time, surrounded by Swedish teenagers. *Surely they were what they seemed?*

Megan was still having her picture taken. This time Adam would have to get off. He let the bus pass the square, now certain that a girl in the distance was Viper, and that no one in the square could be trusted. He stepped off onto the Strand.

Adam didn't notice two white vans passing on a circuit. Nor did he consider the man on the corner selling the *Big Issue*, the man who pressed the send button on his cell when Adam stood in front of him. He also missed the young woman, no more than twenty, who appeared on Adam's right and nodded to a man across the road. The word went out that the boy had arrived.

Adam walked so that a statue hid him from Coron's view, then emerged into the center of the square, twenty yards away from Megan. About fifteen people adjusted their positions. Adam stopped ten paces away and glanced at his watch.

Megan saw him and gasped slightly. Adam looked exhausted and disheveled. "You don't have to do this," she mouthed.

Adam smiled.

At that moment, she raced forward, as did he. Adam's mouth was near to her ear, clearly whispering.

Coron made a sign that no one should move. He and a woman closed in.

"That's enough," he said. "The prophecy is fulfilled. The boy Adam has walked willingly up to me. The Master said that it would be in public." Coron opened his arms, confident and triumphant. "And it cannot be more public than this."

At that instant two things happened: Adam threw himself at Coron, and a hundred pigeons fountained into the air as Megan ran. As Adam was pulled away by two men, Coron calmly instructed those around him: "Let her go."

Where to?

Megan ran to the edge of square by the road, but one of Coron's men was waiting on the other side.

What was her idea?

Then a car stopped, a door opened, Megan dived in and the car pulled away quickly.

Someone spoke into a walkie-talkie: a white van glided to a stop and the side door was flung open. Adam was thrown in, pinned down, and the door was closed. Another van pulled up and people jumped in. Others slipped away into the tube station or down side streets.

The car carrying Megan was lost in the distance.

Inside the van Coron turned to Adam. "Hello, Adam. We meet again." He pressed his hands together and leaned forward.

Adam smiled. "She's safe now. And she will tell the police."

Coron smiled and shook his head. "You're a mere boy. Out of your depth."

Adam frowned. He lunged forward, screaming, pummeling with his fists, until he was restrained and punched repeatedly: after the fifth strike to the head he briefly passed out. It was only then that he was still.

36

Earlier that day: 10:00 a.m.

The door swung open and an unsteady figure spoke. "Well, well, well. Adam Grant—it's been a long time," said Mr. Sterling.

Adam stood in the doorway and raised his hands, as if in surrender. "Please don't call the police. You're the only person who can help me. Can I come in?" He sniffed and ran his hand through his matted hair.

Mr. Sterling glanced behind Adam. "As long as you don't kill me." He chuckled slightly and stepped to one side. "If I live, I'll probably get the sack. Never mind."

Like a cat, Adam slipped past him. Dark smears hung from Adam's eyes, and cuts and blotches gave him the appearance of a neglected Victorian orphan. He was pale from exhaustion and a month spent inside. But his manner was confident. Adam used to be terrified if Mr. Sterling even shuffled past him in a corridor; now he took control. "How's your shoulder?" he asked, looking at the bandage.

"Fine," Mr. Sterling replied. "It's good of you to come out of hiding to visit the sick." He smiled slightly. "I presume this isn't just a courtesy call. Do tell me why you're here." He gestured for Adam to sit.

The house had been smart once, but divorce and drink had made it messy and neglected, without exactly being dirty. A bottle of whisky and a glass sat on a table next to cigarette debris and newspapers. Adam was grateful to get straight to the point. "I need your help."

Mr. Sterling gave Adam a look somewhere between astonishment and amusement. "I'm not going to do anything without understanding what's been going on."

Adam took a deep breath. He had considered telling the whole story, but it sounded completely unbelievable, so he whittled it down. "There's a gang after me. They are *very* dangerous. Murderers. So many terrible things have happened." Tears started to appear in Adam's eyes; he immediately wiped them away. "I can't go to the police. Megan—my friend—she'll die if I do."

For Mr. Sterling, the need for alcohol was a thin but persistent and embracing sensation, like a second skin. He took a sip of whisky, outwardly unfazed by Adam's revelation. "It sounds to me as if you do need help. But I find it hard to believe I can do something the police can't."

Adam was buoyed by hope. "I want you to be in your car, in Trafalgar Square, in front of Nelson's Column, at *exactly* two minutes past five this afternoon. *Exactly*—not a second later. Or earlier."

"Hmmm. And?"

"And if you see Megan, tell her to look where I did."

"Sorry?"

"She'll understand," said Adam. He repeated the words very deliberately: "Look where I did."

Mr. Sterling knew that he had to try. "I think you should hand yourself over to the police right now."

Adam stood up and walked toward the door. "No. And if you try to make me, I will do whatever is necessary to escape." It was an idle threat, though he did have a penknife. "Will you do it?"

"Two minutes past five. Okay."

The whole exchange took only four minutes.

5:02 p.m.

Megan suddenly appeared in the passenger seat of a waiting car.

Adam had whispered to her that Mr. Sterling would be there, but it was not the deputy head who grabbed her with his left hand and pulled her in. It was Chief Inspector Hatfield. Sterling had agonized longer than any adult should, but eventually he had gone to the police.

"What?" gasped Megan.

The chief inspector drove immediately and quickly away from Trafalgar Square, weaving erratically through the traffic.

"Where are we going?" Megan asked.

"Keep quiet. If you try to get out, I will arrest you immediately."

For Megan, forced down in the front seat, everything was a blur of dark sky and the top floors of buildings. They twisted left and right. Before long the car stopped at Gospel Oak Police Station.

The evening that followed was a dreadful haze to Megan. She should have been triumphant with freedom, but she became tangled in her story, confused by the questions.

For a start, she couldn't explain where she had been. No, she hadn't seen the building properly. No, she hadn't been harmed. Yes, she had helped Adam when the police wanted him.

And that was an *offense*. Adam was a criminal, and helping a criminal was *serious*.

Mr. Sterling had tried to help, but had only made it worse: Adam was involved in some sort of gang trouble. The boy had said *gang*.

The questions continued.

"Yes, it was a girl who led me to the van.... Yes, she was about my age...."

The truth was slipping away.

"But there was a cult, and they were going to sacrifice me, and other people."

Megan persisted, but her story was sounding silly, even to her.

"That man is involved in the whole thing!" she said at one point, thrusting her finger in the direction of Chief Inspector Hatfield.

A woman police officer intervened. "Did you see the chief inspector at this house?"

Megan shook her head. "No."

"And where were you held in London?"

"I don't know; I was blindfolded! You're all being stupid!"

At about ten o'clock a very senior officer came in. He announced himself as Assistant Commissioner Cook. Megan could tell by the way everyone sat up that he was important.

"I can *personally* vouch for Chief Inspector Hatfield," he said. "I have worked closely with him for many years and trust him *completely*." Megan's parents nodded. "And I know how easily young boys get caught up in these gang problems. The stabbing and shooting that Adam has committed are only too common, I am afraid."

Megan shouted, "So why was I dragged off the street?"

The assistant commissioner turned to Megan's parents. "I am so sorry that your daughter has become involved in this. I hope that you will all be able to move on now that she has chosen to come back."

"Chosen?" This was all going wrong. Megan put her head in her hands and cried. Just before midnight, she was driven home.

And her life lumbered on, slowly, fractured.

Adam lay with headphones in his ears, his arms tied to the metal frame of a bed. His face was cut and bruised. Viper entered and yanked at the wires. Ugly noises leaked into the room until she pressed a button on an iPod under the bed.

Adam looked away as Viper whispered, "You will regret what you've done and what you are." She grabbed Adam's hair and a fist-shaped area of pain formed on Adam's skull. "That's just a little tugging. Prickly, isn't it? Do you notice how you can't concentrate on anything else? Now, it pleases me to make the pain worse." Viper pulled until her fingers were tightly together. "Understand?"

The pain was much sharper now. Adam held his breath and let out a small groan that turned into "Okay."

Viper let go. "Doesn't that feel good? You must learn to appreciate the absence of pain." She patted his hair down as if he was an animal.

She thrust the headphones out, heard distant cymbal-like sounds, put them back on him and left. Minutes passed to hours: the screams and grotesque descriptions in Adam's ears went on and on. Dorm Thirteen sounds.

37

Sometime in the early hours of Wednesday, December 4, Viper entered Adam's room with two men. She stopped the noise. However hard Adam tried to think of something else, a jumble of horrible images fought to remain in his mind. He pictured a sunny field containing his family and friends.

"You smell of piss. It's time for you to get tidied up," said Viper. "Don't think about trying to escape. You're underground here."

Without warning, Viper hit Adam. Blood dribbled from his lower lip. "That," she said, "is for thinking about escaping. Yes, thoughts are punished here as well." She left the room, laughing. "If you try to escape, or I think you're trying, or even considering it, then worse things will happen."

"Okay."

The two men untied Adam and pushed him into a room opposite. There was no lock on the door, and the toilet was stained. The shower was filthy and the water cold, but there was a thin curtain; being behind two barriers, however slight, gave him a few moments of independence. There was no soap and no towel, so Adam dried himself with his T-shirt. He looked at the wristband that Megan had given him. He thought of his parents. Despair sat heavy in his stomach and his body sagged.

He felt as if he were on a boat surrounded by thousands of miles of empty ocean.

The men stood, arms folded, outside the door.

When he returned to his room there was a black cloak on the bare mattress, which he was told to put on. It stretched down to Adam's feet. He wanted it to be ill-fitting and itchy, but the fabric was warm and comfortable.

The men took Adam into the corridor and turned left, away from the main entrance. They went through a door and down, the light fading with each step. At the bottom a patch of stone floor in front of Adam was dimly lit; he was placed at the very edge, a wall of darkness in front of him. There was a hollow rumbling sound. Then he heard steps recede behind him and light ebbed away as the door slowly shut. There was complete darkness and silence.

Adam didn't move except to raise his hands in front of his face, palms out, instinctively shielding himself in case something flew at him. About two minutes later the rumbling started again. They must be near to the tube line; Adam had heard a similar sort of sound once at Leo's birthday party in the basement of a restaurant. They were eight and had joked about it being a dragon.

After the rumbling Adam heard a slight rustling and a tiny sniff. There was someone or something else down here.

Then a flicker of light: a match had been lit. Faintly, Adam saw a robed figure about eight paces away. It was Viper. She held a match to a candle, then another, and another. After the fourth candle, a second robed figure was vaguely apparent, kneeling at an altar. Adam couldn't see who it was, but the voice was unmistakable. Coron. "Come and join us," he said.

Adam stepped forward. Viper had moved to the stone altar to light two candles, one at either side of a large leather-bound book. She moved on to light other candles, thirteen in total.

Coron gestured for Adam to kneel. Adam resisted for a few seconds, then eased himself down on Coron's left. He saw Viper smile as she returned to Coron's right.

"Adam," Coron started, "we are a special trinity. I will be Lord; Viper is the best of my disciples; you are the sacrifice, appearing again after two thousand years. In the world, there are no others like us. The universe is a play: we are the main characters. The Master has spoken. Go ahead and read." Coron indicated for Adam to look at the book.

Adam stood up and approached the altar as another rumbling passed underneath them. The book contained small handwritten lines, hundreds of words on each page—hundreds of thousands of words in total. Adam glanced at one line in the middle: "The blood from his hands will flow like merciless streams...." Then, a few pages on, another line: "She will serve Lord Coron with a love that is ocean deep...."

The same words appeared over and over: *blood, sacrifice, death, pain, service, love*... A lot of the phrases were similar; it was an obsessive outpouring of insanity. Page after page after page.

"Turn to the beginning," said Coron.

Adam flicked back, and several times, near the bottom of the first page, he saw a name in the margin. His name. He turned to the very last page: "Adam." At the top of the last page: "Adam, a willing sacrifice..." Sometimes his name was in capitals. He flicked back. "ADAM is a sack of filth that will burst open if he becomes fourteen." It was rambling, inconsistent, bizarre. The words seemed to spill from the pages and float in front of his eyes.

Adam was thinking about tearing the book up, or tipping a candle onto it, when Coron called him back: "Come and kneel before the Master."

Adam returned, his mind needled by the phrase *willing sacrifice*. He knelt.

There was silence, and then Coron boomed, as if in triumph, "The Master is here. Let us listen."

Adam glanced across. Coron and Viper had both closed their eyes.

Coron saw burning pebble eyes, a wrinkled face and a thin, cloaked body. He heard the Master speak: "Well done, Coron. You have served me well by bringing the boy here."

"Thank you, Master," said Coron.

"I hear him," said Adam.

Sound again welled up in Coron's ears. "The boy must serve me. He must be a willing sacrifice. He must become one of us."

"Yes, he will," said Coron.

"Yes," added Adam.

Coron turned to Adam, eyes half open. "Can you see the Master?"

"No," said Adam confidently, "but I heard him." He thought frantically for something he had read on the last page of Coron's book, hoping to deceive him. "He says that I must be a willing sacrifice."

Viper frowned. "Lord Coron, he mocks us."

"No," said Coron, excited. "He has repeated the words of the Master. He did hear."

The Later Days

In Adam's room *The Great Book* was laid out on a table. Some sentences had been written out tens of times in pen, like lines set as a punishment at school. Others had been copied and decorated, and about ten were taped to the wall. Soon the room was papered with quotations from Coron's book.

Adam had even drawn a picture of the place of his sacrifice: it was a very tall triangular-shaped building that tapered away to nothing. It looked like a shard of glass.

Many times, Coron entered and smiled in his deranged way. *A willing sacrifice indeed.*

On one occasion, Adam knelt next to Coron, his eyelids pressed tightly shut as he said, "Master: make me the perfect sacrifice. As it says in your book, 'lambs are slaughtered just like sheep.' And raise up Lord Coron." Adam's arms were outstretched. "Let the world see the moment of my surrender." Coron was manically energetic despite an almost complete lack of sleep: he gave a high-pitched ecstatic howl. *A willing sacrifice indeed.*

On Wednesday, December 25, Viper sat, catlike, on Adam's bed while he leaned against the wall.

"How did it feel to kill in the service of the Master?" Adam asked.

"I enjoyed it," she said airily. "Just as any hunter enjoys killing prey." Then, blandly, openly, chillingly, "God makes it enjoyable so that we are enthusiastic for our work."

"What about Simon, your brother?"

Viper looked deep into Adam's eyes. "Sidewinder made it happen. I was ashamed of him. I enjoyed the power I had to extinguish him." She leaned forward. "You almost had a sister: Megan. She has left you alone here. Betrayed you. After all that you had done for her. And you are forgotten. Now she spends her time with other boys. Laughing with them. Leaning against them. Kissing them. Just imagine if you had a chance to avenge that betrayal."

"Yes," said Adam. "I can imagine it."

The attempt at brainwashing continued day after day after day after day.

Hour after hour after hour.

Minute by minute.

Every second.

38

Hatfield pushed Adam against a wall in his room, dislodging a couple of the sheets of paper. "Your friend Megan has been reported missing. Vanished into thin air."

Adam seemed interested rather than worried. "Is she here? It would be glorious if she could join The People."

Hatfield paused and eyed Adam carefully. "No. She has evaporated. Her parents are mystified and banging on the police station door. As are yours still. Your parents are eaten up with grief, you know that?"

"My parents don't understand about The People. And they're not my *real* parents anyway. True parents would be proud that my sacrifice ushers in the new kingdom."

Hatfield's manner eased slightly. "Do you know anything about Megan's disappearance?"

"I think I should speak to Lord Coron and the Master."

At that instant the door opened. "And as if by magic, we are both here." Coron's head jerked from side to side. He was much thinner, even gaunt; his hollow eyes stared at Adam. "We want to know what this means." Coron now always used *we*. "Tell us about Megan."

Adam leaned forward. "In *The Great Book* it says that the

energy of sacrifice strengthens even God." Adam returned Coron's stare. "Megan's sacrifice will strengthen me." Adam paused, bitterness tightening his mouth. "Why should she live? Why? When I am here because of her."

Coron pulled his arms in close to his body and bellowed. "The Master is within me. And you are my wise son. Just as the old god sacrificed his son, so I will sacrifice you!"

Adam reached out and rested his hand on Coron's shoulder. His words reflected the style of *The Great Book*: "I am indeed your son. Let us find Megan together."

This could work, thought Adam. *This* will *work—if Megan has read my letter.*

About an hour later, Hatfield reappeared. He paused before speaking, looking from Adam's left eye to his right and back again. "Get in the shower," he said, almost under his breath.

Adam had learned to endure the cold, but this time he heard the outer door open while he cleaned himself as best he could. Adam feared it was Viper, so shielded himself with the curtain and peered out. But it was Hatfield, who wouldn't hurt him without Coron's permission.

"I've brought you a towel," said the chief inspector. "And a change of clothes. We wouldn't want anything carried out of this building." Hatfield picked up everything—socks, boxer shorts, jeans, T-shirt and sweatshirt—and left a pile of fresh clothes.

"Keep a gun to my back, Mr. Hatfield. It is only wise that you make sure I don't return to my old ways. I have nothing to fear."

Adam put on the new clothes and was guided away from his room and upstairs. This was the first time he had been above ground in three weeks.

He immediately realized what a busy building it was. Coron's writings contained vast amounts of information about his plans, the carnage that explosions would cause, and the nature and location of Adam's sacrifice, but there was nothing about the numbers of people involved. There were easily thirty or forty people around, possibly more.

"Any second thoughts?" Hatfield asked Adam as he stood next to Coron.

"No. I will lead you to her."

"If you shout once that door is open," said Hatfield, "you will get about two words out."

Ignoring Hatfield, Adam spoke to Coron. "Lord Coron. I will not do these things."

Viper draped a backpack over her back. "I am very excited at the prospect of Megan's return. Very excited. Just as you have changed, so will the world."

Adam walked to the car with his head down and meekly directed the driver to the right address by the quickest route. Hatfield sat on his right and Viper on his left, with Coron in the passenger seat. Two men and two women were in the car behind.

The driver pulled up on the same side as Simon's flat, and the other car stopped directly across the road.

Adam eased himself from the car and walked quickly toward the door, Coron, Viper and Hatfield coming with him. Adam didn't turn to see the others take up positions in the street.

Hatfield nodded and smiled as he saw which building Adam was leading them to. He glanced across to the park. *So Adam had been here the whole time,* he thought.

They climbed four flights of stairs: fifty-two steps. When they reached the door to the flat, Megan was less than twenty-feet away.

Hatfield nudged past Adam and struck at the lock with a hammer and chisel, then pushed a thick piece of wire inside.

A door opened downstairs, and a head appeared at the bottom of the last flight of stairs. "What's going on, man?"

Chief Inspector Hatfield immediately responded. "Police. And if you don't get back in your room I'll send some of the drug-squad boys around to investigate that smell."

There was muttering and the sound of a closing door. And the door to Simon's old flat swung open.

"Go ahead," Coron whispered, leaning very close to Adam's ear.

Adam stood in the doorway.

"Step in."

Adam walked in, two paces ahead of the others.

There was no sound, just the ticking of a clock. Time slipping away.

Coron was barely audible now. "Call for Megan," he mouthed.

"Megan. Megan?"

"Say, 'It is Adam.' "

"Megan, it's Adam."

"Say you are alone."

"I'm alone, Megan."

"Tell her to come out. And louder. Say that everything is all right."

Adam spoke louder. "Megan, you can come out. Everything is all right. You know you can trust me."

Nothing.

The other three joined Adam in the flat.

Adam turned. "I don't think she's here."

Coron spoke slightly louder this time. "Try again. Tell her that you've escaped. Say that you promise."

"Megan. Listen. I've escaped. Megan?" Adam shrugged. "She really isn't here." Then to himself, "Where is she?"

Megan heard everything.

The other three moved into the flat. Hatfield went to the table where London maps and tube printouts were scattered, holding them up for everyone to see. Viper went toward the kitchen and Coron into the bedroom. After a few minutes they were sure Megan was not there.

"Tear this place apart," said Coron, wringing his hands aggressively, twitchy with nervous energy. "The Master wants to be certain she isn't here."

"She must be out," said Adam. "You could put a man outside to catch her when she returns."

"I'd thought of that," said Hatfield. "We'll get her, don't worry."

After the possible hiding places had been ruled out, there was a search: Simon's few books were flicked through, the bed was cut open, the underside of drawers checked—every possible place examined.

Adam took a glass and poured a drink, offering one to the others. Hatfield scowled. Viper accepted. She held up faded cushions for Hatfield to cut into with a penknife. Finally Adam pointed up to a door in the sitting-room ceiling.

Hatfield raised his eyebrows. He stood on a kitchen chair and eased up the hatch. "Flashlight?"

Adam spotted one on a shelf that contained lots of odds and ends. He fumbled about getting it and switched it on. Hatfield pushed his head through to the loft space and shone the flight-light around. "Nothing."

Adam headed to the bathroom.

"Hey, where are you going?" said Hatfield, jumping down off the stool.

"For a piss. You can stand next to me and have a look if you like. I'll leave the door open."

Viper smiled as Adam passed.

Megan held her breath.

For about ten seconds there was the sound of Adam spraying into toilet water. Hatfield looked through the door twice at the distinctive shape of a young man urinating.

"Let's go," said Coron. "I'm going to send someone up here to wait for her return. Also, check whether she's back with her parents. We want her, don't we, Adam." It was a statement, not a question.

They left, Hatfield taking one last look around before he closed the door.

In two days Adam was going to be sacrificed.

39

SUNDAY, DECEMBER 29, TO TUESDAY, DECEMBER 31, 2013

Megan heard the door close. In the ceiling of Simon's spare bedroom was the thin outline of a square hatch, and above the hatch crouched Megan, ready to swing a frying pan. She dared to breathe again.

Had they actually gone?

She listened for her name. Nothing. *Megan*—Adam had never called her that in her life, except to impersonate her parents. For years it was *Meggie* and now always *Meg. Megan*— never. Adam's appearance made the situation clear: he couldn't escape, he couldn't send a message from where he was and lives were at risk. *Can it really have come down to us?*

Megan pushed the hatch down an inch. She glimpsed a torn duvet and the bottom of the half-open door. Widening the gap another couple of inches, she saw drawers in an erratic jumble and a ripped mattress. Then, even more: the bedside cabinet upside down and the lamp smashed.

Megan could hear children shrieking in the park and the angry squeal of a passing motorcycle. Otherwise there was silence.

She had to move quickly. If Adam had left a message, she knew where it would be. Adam had whispered two things to her in Trafalgar Square: one was about running for the car, the other to "go to where we went through water." And there Megan had found what Adam had hurriedly left for her: a letter, directions, money and the keys to Simon's flat. Adam had written his messages in a scruffy and poorly spelled scrawl, including "IF I CAN I WILL LEAVE A MESSAGE IN THE CESTERN ABOVE THE TOILET."

Now Megan eased the collapsible ladder down as gently as she could, but it clattered the last eighteen inches. She froze. By now they would be outside, and Coron would be instructing someone to return. And if Megan could have heard, she would have caught the words "kill her if necessary."

Kill her echoed menacingly in Adam's head as he glanced back up at the building. The upstairs windows stared back like inky-black eyes.

Before, the ladder had squeaked as she used it, but now the noise sounded like a train clattering through a station. Megan jumped the last four steps.

Thud.

After every noise she feared someone bursting in, but the man sent to wait for her was still behind the dark windows of the Range Rover, concealing a gun inside his coat. As Megan rushed into the bathroom, he closed the car door and raised a hand in farewell to Coron.

Megan lifted the lid to the cistern, but there was nothing hidden inside. *Perhaps a piece of paper had floated behind the mechanism?* Nothing. She looked into the toilet itself—nothing. *Why had Adam come? Why take the risk and then not leave anything?*

On hands and knees she examined behind the toilet.

Nothing.

Adam!

The man was opening the main door to the building, just fifty-two steps away.

Megan sat down on the edge of the bath, frowning with concentration as her eyes darted everywhere. It was then that she saw the toilet roll next to her. Just visible, nosing out from inside, was a red wristband.

A message had been written around the inside: "Top of shard midnight 31st. Bombs planned. HELP. Love AG."

The man had trudged up the first two flights of stairs.

Megan grabbed the wristband and ran. She scurried up the ten metal steps two at a time, the noise filling the flat: *clink, clatter, crash, clang, clank.*

Outside, the man had one flight of stairs to go: thirteen steps.

Megan pulled the ladder up, three tugs on the rope making a rumbling rattle of noise.

Megan froze.

After a few seconds, she heard shuffling sounds. Someone was downstairs. Then she realized the utter silence around her: the hum of the fridge had stopped and the computer was lifeless. There were only three electrical appliances in the loft—a small fridge, a laptop and a single bulb in the center of the main room—and all were fed off one socket from below. She imagined the plug loose or pulled out. If only she had known. *If only...*

Using a flashlight, crawling across the loft room, she moved to Simon's bedroom area, made cell-like by the sloping roof. It was almost certainly above a different flat, but it was hard to work out the distances. *If only* she had a drill that could cut a hole...in silence...and without the need for electricity.

It was hopeless. Even if she broke through the tiles, there was an enormous and fatal drop. Megan considered tying together sheets from the bed. She didn't have enough sheets, the knots would never hold, and even if they did she would have to rappel down without a harness or safety net. *If only* there was a fire escape.

She thought of Adam's message again, closed her eyes and let out a quiet, desperate sigh.

She would have to wait. But her guards were equally patient.

The voices changed, sometimes one, sometimes two, but every hour she faintly heard a telephone call sent from the flat below. Megan slept in short bursts. She silently plucked what she could from the tiny fridge but dared not light the gas stove. Then she turned to cornflakes straight from the box. She silently sucked them one at a time by flashlight, careful not to make any noise.

She always hoped that the next hour would bring silence downstairs. It never did.

Time slipped by. Twelve, then twenty-four, then forty-eight long hours. Adam's death crept closer. She was desperate. In less than twenty-four hours it would be the New Year.

Adam thought about holding Coron and Hatfield down and punching them. He could imagine punching a bully like Jake, but only if he lost his temper or had to, and he winced at the idea of kicking someone who was helpless. But it was different with these two men: if the time came, he would not go quietly.

But he must not let Coron know this.

Adam grew more and more ambitious in his show of devotion to the Master: he went into trances, threw himself to the floor and even acted as the Master's mouthpiece by spouting lines from Coron's book. He scratched his own chest, leaving crude red etchings, which he claimed were a punishment, and, on one occasion, a message. Dribbling, he gave a frenzy of praise to Coron, whose devotion to the Master did not prevent an enjoyment of personal flattery that was close to worship.

Adam was thinking of how to exploit the trust he had earned, probably by claiming that the Master did not actually want his death, when Viper came in.

Adam hated Viper as well, but he couldn't imagine hurting her in the same way. He knew that she was as evil as them, and she had a fondness for small acts of cruelty that went beyond theirs, but this inner darkness was wrapped in beauty. Whenever she pretended to be friendly, Adam found himself wanting to forgive her. He couldn't help himself.

She came in and sat on his bed, the door still open. "We still can't find your old friend. Any ideas?"

Adam didn't answer.

"Do you prefer her to me?"

"You know that I like you." Adam was not entirely lying.

Viper took his right hand and put it on her shoulder, guiding it up to her neck. She then picked up his other hand and smiled. "This is your chance to kiss me."

Adam looked at her eyes and lips. Beauty is the most powerful mask.

Then Viper pushed him away, but let her hand linger on his chest for a moment. *It's all a game to her,* Adam thought.

"Where is that red band, the one around your wrist?" she said.

"I lost it," Adam said.

"Where?"

"It must have dropped off." He shrugged. "Maybe it's under the bed."

"I've seen you touching it and looking at it. I think it came from Megan, or possibly your parents. Why would you *lose* it now?"

Adam had to say it, though it sounded to him like the crap it was. "I'm more interested in the Master and serving him."

The house was very busy as the New Year approached. Viper shouted for someone passing to ask Lord Coron to come. She was the only person who would dare do such a thing.

Adam made a play of searching for the band and Viper looked briefly in the shower room opposite. Within a few minutes Coron joined them. He no longer needed to conjure the Master up; he believed him present all of the time, as real as any person.

"I think," said Viper, standing next to Coron, "that this boy may be cleverer than we give him credit for. I think he may have left something when we went on our little trip."

Adam stood, shouting, "Lord Coron, check with the Master.

I have lost a mere...thing, a thing that doesn't mean anything to me. I have the Master to think about, and that I'm going to be killed."

"I don't like your shouting. It's *killed*, is it? I thought it was *sacrificed*. The Master is shaking his head." Coron was unable to stand still.

"I meant sacrificed," Adam said. *Don't look guilty.*

Coron turned to Viper. "Get them to have another good look around that flat. See if there is a dropped wristband. And I think Adam can stay here and prepare himself for his *sacrifice*."

The men in Simon's flat did eight-hour shifts, frustrated that they had not been able to please Lord Coron and the Master. The tools of capture were waiting, including handcuffs and tape.

The message came to check the flat thoroughly again, an order, it was said, from the Master himself. As day slid into evening, the man on duty took three hours to minutely examine the property: first the sitting room and kitchen, then the bathroom, then the bedroom.

A plug lay on the floor under the bed. With finger and thumb he followed the cable until it snaked under the carpet.... Then he ripped up the tacks....He followed the wire as it ran above the floorboards and up the wall, behind a cheap plastic cover....And disappeared into the ceiling.

Looking up, he frowned: there was a thin outline of a square in the ceiling. The loft had been checked, but the Master's instructions were clear—and the Master might be watching. Teetering on the edge of the bed, he scraped at the hatch, but it wouldn't open.

Up in the loft, Megan heard scuffing. *Oh my God.*

The man fetched a chair and shoved twice with his hands. The lock suddenly gave away: the hatch squeaked up and then down, and a ladder appeared. He dragged it down and wandered back to get the flashlight.

Megan saw his head appear, tortoise-like, lit from underneath. She hesitated. *It's his head! This is one of the worst moments in my life.* Then the consequences of being caught burst into her mind.

The man pushed the torch through the top of the gap. "What the...?"

He shone the torch around the room: a small fridge, a chair—hell! He saw sneakers and jeans.

Megan brought the frying pan crashing down with all her strength. She expected there to be a sickening crunch and thud instead of a bonging sound. Then there was a rush of noise as the man fell down the steps of the ladder. He lay on the floor, groaning and confused, but certainly alive.

Megan scuttled down the ladder as the man raised himself up off the carpet like a lumbering sea monster. She had to do it again. This time there was an uglier sound, and there was blood: Megan could see a steady trickle running from the man's misshapen nose and onto the floor. He was not moving; perhaps he was dead.

She grabbed his flashlight, avoiding his gun—a gun!—and quickly went back up the steps, collecting her coat and with it the bits and pieces she had prepared during her long wait. She stepped over the man, avoiding the blood. He let out a tiny moan.

Megan knew what she was going to do. There was a police station about five streets away on the western side of the park. She would go there and explain the situation: then the police would find the man in the flat and see his gun. *Thank God it is almost over,* Megan thought. *Adults can get involved.*

Megan jogged, passing only two people. It was a chilly night best spent inside. With two streets to go, she waited to let a taxi and a minibus pass before crossing an intersection. The man in the newsagent's opposite was closing up, collecting a metal board. Megan could see the headline: "'Kidnap' Girl Wanted in Connection with Murders."

She raced across. Inside the door on the right were a few

papers that hadn't sold. Megan's picture was clearly on the front. Inspector Hatfield was prominently featured, as well as an assistant commissioner. The police were saying that she was on the run with Adam; she could see the phrase "a young Bonnie and Clyde," attributed to Hatfield. There was a shaded box underneath, with the title "When Children Kill Children."

She dropped the paper and ran.

40

Coron showed Adam his hands. "Look—they're bleeding again. Just like thirteen years ago. But this time the blood will water our new kingdom. And not only my blood. Yours!" He leaned forward as he laughed softly. "And the blood of others. Those who do not celebrate the Master but celebrate your birthday."

"They're just enjoying themselves. It has nothing to do with me, you mental bastard. It's New Year's. No one knows or cares that this is my birthday. You're insane." Adam had given up his pretense and was tied to the bed again. They had worked out that somehow he had helped Megan.

"I would like to damage you," said Coron, "for your deception. But you will be lifted up in front of all of London as the perfect sacrifice. At the moment you become an adult, after twelve strikes of the bell, the blood will pour from your body."

Adam carried on. "People will never follow an evil nutter like you. People are good."

Coron laughed hysterically. "Three hours."

Viper walked in.

"Here's another bloody lunatic," shouted Adam, straining to get up.

Coron grabbed Adam's lips so that he couldn't speak. He leaned forward and spoke quietly. "I will be on the mountaintop with you. Viper will also be there. She has the honor of pressing the button that will set London ablaze. Thirteen *so-called* landmarks, all destroyed. This city will never be the same again. Out of this will arise my kingdom. It is written."

Adam roared through Coron's tightening hands.

"Go on—cry out! We have been planning tonight for two years. Twelve different locations, and you will be at the thirteenth. It will happen. IT IS WRITTEN."

Hatfield was responsible for binding Adam so that he couldn't escape. Adam struggled; it took four men to cuff his hands in front of him and wrap tape over his mouth and around the back of his head. Death had now cast its fearful shadow over him. Adam certainly would have shouted and screamed if he could.

He was thrown to the floor and rolled over and over as a thick carpet encircled him. Adam wriggled, but it was like being wedged inside a pipe. Then he felt his head dip as he went down steps. Revelers cavorted past, waving their arms and cheering, unaware that four men were dropping a boy into the back of a van. Adam made a deep humming sound, something like an animal in pain; no one was listening.

The van drove across London through happy, oblivious crowds, followed by a Range Rover. Coron smiled as he considered how the bombs and receivers had gone into place: one nudged behind the bell mechanism in Big Ben by a man leading a tour group, another slid under a table in Buckingham Palace by a woman with a vacuum cleaner, a third left tied to the outside of Tower Bridge by a man polishing windows....Twelve dull white packages and wires linked to a receiver.

Coron tapped the transmitter in his hand and passed it to Viper. "You may have the honor," he said. She smiled.

Adam could twist slightly inside his cocoon, but no more. Fear rose inside him: *I don't want to die. I'm so young. I'm good, I'm kind. Why me?*

And anger: *Maybe I should have done things differently.*

*Maybe I could have run. Why couldn't Simon kill Coron? Why did
I try to rescue Megan and save my parents? Why doesn't someone
care enough to rescue me? Why did my real mother give me away?
Why me?*

A little hope: *Surely there will be someone I can call to. Surely
I will have a chance to run away. Surely I won't die.*

Adam felt the slope as they dipped into a car park underneath the tallest building in London. Then he was being moved
again, dragged from the van and carried sideways for a couple
of minutes. Then upright for about twenty seconds. There was
a tiny jolt. A lift? He could hear a whirring noise. Then carried
sideways for a short time and upright again for longer—another
lift? After further movement he felt himself toppling over and
landed on his left shoulder. He wriggled slightly, then lay still,
listening, the carpet pressed against his nose.

He could hear the sound of voices, and of glass being
smashed. Then he was nudged with a foot and the carpet
unrolled, tumbling him out on to a wooden floor.

Wind howled into the large, bare apartment, blowing
tiny flecks of glass across the floor. Coron stood where the
floor-to-ceiling window would have been, a sledgehammer at
his feet. Two long ropes, about six feet apart, dangled out of the
window, attached at one end to metal supports in the ceiling.
"Welcome to the mountain," he said. The wind blew his hair
erratically, making it writhe like snakes.

Adam noticed the transmitter in Viper's hand.

"Yes," she said. "Midnight. Six minutes."

Outside the apartment, a guard stood with his arms folded. He
looked toward the window at the end of the corridor, city lights
twinkling below, the London Eye slowly edging around. *Tonight
the world changes,* he thought. Then, reflected in the window,
the man saw the outline of a small person holding a gun.

He heard a sound and there was a searing pain in his lower
back. His left hand returned covered in crimson. *Blood?* He

found himself being barged over, and his hands were pulled back and cuffed. Blood seeped from his side. He choked slightly, trying to speak.

Megan's voice, trying to sound far more confident than she was: "The second bullet *will* kill you, so don't move."

He saw sneakers and jeans step toward the fire alarm and smash the glass. Then the door behind him opened. Megan had taken his keys.

Adam was hauled to his feet and pushed forward toward the open window. Viper drew little shapes on the side of his neck with a knife as Coron tied Adam's wrists together with plastic cord and then added rope, in addition to the handcuffs.

Coron held Adam's hands above his head, making a distorted and elongated O-shape. Then, smiling, he picked up one of two ropes tied to metal beams above ripped-out ceiling tiles. Adam understood when he saw the metallic clip at the end. It was just like one that would attach to a harness: he was going to thread the rope through the "O" made by Adam's arms and clip it back up in a loop. They were going to dangle Adam out of the smashed window. He remembered the silhouette Simon and he had seen against the side of the Old School House, that terrible night. Had that been in anticipation of this?

Adam snarled at Coron, "Get off me, you idiot!"

"The rope won't kill you," said Coron. "But this knife will. Then the Master will be free to rule." Coron's eyes were wide and wild. "Here we are at last: Lord, Disciple and Sacrifice. We are the trinity at the center of the universe."

Adam was linked on to one of the dangling ropes. Coron picked up the other.

Viper looked at her watch. "Two minutes," she said, handing the knife to Coron and moving to the other side of the window. She pulled out the transmitter.

There was a crunch of glass. "STOP!" Viper and Coron

turned. It was Megan, holding the gun she had taken from the man in Simon's flat. "Stop right there, and put everything down."

Coron held the knife to Adam's neck. Viper held the transmitter in her hand. For a moment no one moved or spoke.

Then it was Coron. "It seems you have a choice. You can *try* to shoot Viper and stop her pressing a button that will set London ablaze, or you can *try* to shoot me to prevent me killing Adam. Your choice. Either way, I doubt you have much experience with guns."

"I fired it three times in the flat when I went back to pick it up, and once just now into your security guard's back. I know that the bullet goes where I point the gun."

Viper laughed aloud. "A choice. Trick or treat?"

It was a few seconds to midnight. In the distance, Big Ben made its usual sixteen musical chimes before ringing for the hour. Megan looked between the two possible targets, unsure that she could hit either.

In the pause before the first bong, Megan pulled the trigger: Viper was hit in the arm, little more than a graze, but the transmitter spun from her hands and came to rest on the edge of the open window space.

Adam kicked out at Coron's shins and kneed him in the balls, forcing him toward the edge with each blow. Toppling back, Coron grabbed at Adam with his right hand and kept hold of the remaining rope with his left, pulling both of them from the building. Adam's arms jolted in their sockets as he stopped about fifteen feet below the window, dangling nine hundred feet above London. Coron slipped down his own rope, struggling to get a hold, slightly farther down.

The deep sounds of Big Ben rang out.

Ignoring her injury, Viper leaped for the transmitter, and Megan ran toward her. On the second chime, Viper picked up the device, London as her backdrop, and on the third she stood and turned.

Four. Megan thumped her hard in the face. Viper edged back a little, inches from the drop, wind roaring past her.

Adam and Coron dangled outside the building, trying to hold on, each attempting to kick out at the other.

Five. Megan's right fist made contact with Viper's cheek. "Don't!"

Viper edged a little farther back.

Six. Megan's left fist pounded Viper's stomach. "Play trick or treat!"

Viper struggled to press the button, missing once, twice.

Seven. Megan's right hand hit Viper's mouth as hard as she could. "With me!"

Eight. Viper overbalanced on the edge of the building, arms waving, and fell back, the transmitter spilling from her hand.

Two policemen were sitting in their car below, listening to the chimes, when seconds later—*smash!*—something heavy landed on their roof. "Bloody hell!"

Nine. Adam swung himself across and kicked one foot at Coron.

Ten. Adam kicked out with both feet, his clip and ropes creaking and stretching.

Megan watched from above.

Eleven. Adam swung across again, but Coron grabbed his left foot and spun him around. If Coron was going to fall, he would take Adam with him.

Twelve. Adam's right foot connected with Coron's face.

An instant later, Coron's hand slipped from the rope.

For a moment before he fell, Coron's feet seemed to catch against the building and he defied gravity. New Year fireworks sparkled in his black eyes.

Adam saw him mouth one word:

"Thirteen."

And with the next heartbeat, Adam became fourteen years old.

epilogue

The government inquiry into the events of New Year's Eve, 2013, known as the Kirby Report after the lead judge, took almost four months.

Adam, Megan and their parents had been invited into Judge Kirby's office in advance of the publication of his report. After outlining its contents, he tapped the document, which ran to nearly a thousand closely typed pages. "There's significant legal talk in here. There have been a lot of failures. But one thing that comes through clearly is how brave you have been. Adam, I don't know how you managed to keep your mind. You're a remarkable young man."

Adam glanced down, embarrassed. "Thank you."

Judge Kirby stood up and adjusted his blazer. "And now I have to present this to the press. I wish I could publicly congratulate you, but in this document you are Child A, and you, Megan, are Child B. How are you going to celebrate?"

Adam paused for a second. "Well, I want to hang out with my friends," he said. He smiled and stood a bit closer to Megan. "I never did have a birthday party."

That evening, surrounded by pizza and Coke in a real Italian restaurant, he did, with Asa, Leo, Rachel and Megan. Near the end, Asa stood up and coughed in mock seriousness. "Adam and Megan, we salute you!" Coke spilled from his cup.

Adam laughed and bowed a little, looking at Megan. Then he was serious and looked at the flickering candle in the middle of the table. *Thank God it's all over.*

Thank God it's all over!

At the same moment, at the top of a castle far away, another candle flickered, casting a cold, thin light.

It illuminated the turning pages of a leather-bound book.

In a chamber, underneath the castle, a girl tapped on the thick glass of the container that imprisoned her. "Help me, please!" She tapped again. "Please, help me!"

But there was no one to help.

appendix

CULTS DO EXIST

Cult: *(noun)* A relatively small group of people having religious beliefs or practices regarded by others as strange or as imposing excessive control over members.
—*Oxford English Dictionary*

In 1971 cult leader Charles Manson was convicted of encouraging his followers to commit murders inspired by songs from the Beatles' *White Album.*

In 1978 Jim Jones killed 914 people, including 200 children and an American congressman, at his camp, called Jonestown, in Guyana, on the northern coast of South America.

In 1994, after a fifty-one-day standoff with police at his compound in Texas, seventy-six members of David Koresh's Branch Davidian cult died in a fire.

Also in 1994 fifty-three members of the wealthy Solar Temple cult were killed at their base outside Geneva, Switzerland. One cult member had earlier stabbed his three-month-old son to death in the belief that the baby was going to harm the group leader.

The People, however, do not exist.